PLAYGROUND

PLAYGROUND is the first novel by Dave Attrill, in a series
based around the cases of maverick Sheffield detective duo
Leyton
and Garstone.

TITLES TO FOLLOW:

FIONA *

THREE STRIKES

VANS

VICTIMLESS CRIMES

See endpaper for further synopsis of this next release.

Thanks to my family and all friends who have supported and encouraged me along the way, Beverley, David, Krissy, Dave, Chris and all other who have offered me advice and assistance at various stages, and largely to the many who have put up with me talking non-stop about the project, every time we meet.

Published by lulu.com 2011.

Front and rear cover by author.

1

STRANGE DEATH, STRANGER MEN

(i)

The freezing autumn air over the village seemed to make the morning daylight descend significantly slower. Whilst normally it was at least reasonably light, 7:15 a.m. on a typical October day, the tangerine glare of the street lights, combined with lingering mist from the previous night, kept the sky at its darkest till the last moment possible.

Only the regular dozen pigeons grouping for their daily pavement breakfast on Devonshire Road encroached the stillness, their peace itself broken in turn by the Co-op store behind them raising its shutter. The young student assistant's emergence scared at least half the flock off the concrete - those few left too besotted by their breadcrusts to care.

As the supermarket front lit its many green and white windows, the banquet remained uninterrupted, until a second human intruder approached to bypass their space.

The tracksuit clad shape disappeared behind the bus shelter opposite. Wearing a dark woolly hat, at a horrendously lopsided angle, he strangely ignored the friendly "Ayup mate!" from the assistant, a pleasantry that he would normally turn aside to exchange.

This second young male appeared dedicated to defying the cold that his insufficiently thin zip jacket yielded him to feeling. Robbie accelerated his Olympic-style gallop over the kerb, continuing away into the fog. Coming to the end of the street, and its treacherously narrow, potholed pavement he saw nearly the entire row of local shops light up across the main road.

The village newsagents appeared to be springing into activity as well. Allowing for a breath and for traffic, he galloped across the road via the bollards aiming directly at his usual early-morning oasis.

Robbie could almost taste that Orange Smoothie as he reached the door of the newsagents. A somewhat mentally challenged individual, he was confused to find the door fully locked and the shop only partly lit inside.

(This can't be right; it's always open when I've got here.)

A tall shape came towards the window inside, that of Val the shop owner - always a person he looked forward to seeing. The feeling didn't appear mutual today.

'*We're shut, love*" he lip-read the woman shouting, as she fingered the opening hours out to him. "*Can't you read*?"

TUE 7:30 - 6:00   the entry for today read.

That's the time I normally get here. Robbie backed away, developing aggressive self-pity, the possible symptom of some kind of mental imbalance. (*Am I stupid?)* he chuntered to himself.   (*Not got the brain to come here at the right time?)* Churned into an aggressive frenzy, he tottered aimlessly up the pavement, feeling bizarrely small towards himself. He didn't know entirely why. (*Am I stupid, was I born yesterday? That retarded I don't learn what time the newsagent's opens?)*

A high-pitched hooter caught him off guard, just straying within

4

two metres of an incoming No30. Robbie dived away, just managing to collect the obscenities launched at him by its over-irate driver. Made to feel only more lessened in self-esteem, he forced himself not to take it to heart.

There did seem to be a lesson to learn from taking his jog twenty minutes earlier than usual; the world was maybe twenty minutes less ready to receive him. Setting his alarm for an ungodlier hour hadn't been such a bright idea - he'd have time for a longer run, but with the near death experience just encountered it would be wise to turn towards home and call it a morning.

(Could cut through to Townhead Road: finish my run off there instead). This came over as a good thought. Dive down through the gennel, getting away from that lovely 'bus bloke' who might just maintain his vow to run Robbie into the ground next time they met.

The past few minutes' fiasco hadn't turned the sky any lighter so, using the amber glow as his guide Robbie resumed his leisurely turkey-trot-like run, heading along the cul-de-sac. A large double-mesh gate to the village football club made the end of the short street easy to see, the concealed alley's entrance sat exactly two houses from the end.

Robbie counted past the semi-detacheds two-by-two, spotting the green 'Footpath' sign lurking closer in the gloom. As he reached his turn-off, there was something off-kilter about the gate, that stopped him in his tracks.

Though the kid only ventured by this route about once a fortnight, that was still frequent enough to understand the facility as being locked from public use on a weekday - the local clubs only visited this pitch on Sunday afternoons during the autumn, bar the odd charity game (he should know, he played in them).

The two halves sat prised apart by a good foot, the padlocked chain, stretched to its limit clearly the only thing to have delayed an intruder. Robbie realised that climbing through into the ground would make him appear as equal a trespasser in his own right, yet as a fully fledged member and friend of the home squad, he felt it his duty to protect their turf.

Not exactly skilled in avoiding action, Robbie caught the chain with the tip of his hat as he ducked below. Though only a faint tinkle, it did set his hair on end for the moment. *Best to get into the dark bit*, he thought, climbing round against the hedge. Out of the streetlamp glow that could no longer spotlight him, he had only the CCTV left to get round.

Keeping tightly to the edge of the grass, he monitored the lone camera on the pavilion roof more attentively than it did him. He wasn't the brightest tool in the kit but was used to the way it rotated slowly anti-clockwise then back. Sitting on its gargoyle-like perch at the corner of the building, it didn't worry Robbie too easily; he just had to keep his slither a step ahead.

Whilst it seemed more interested in the roof of the church hall next door, he cooled his wits and crept along the embankment, following the tracks trodden in by countless team buses over the years.

(Shit!)

A vehicle motor was audible from not too afar. He dived back under the hedge and looked. A flicker of red light passed behind the trees.

(Who's got a car in the 'Rec'?) Robbie noticed the lights were coming, or possibly going, from the neighbouring park.

6

Checking to see what the camera was doing, it was almost trained on him, save about five degrees. Crouched low on the tracks, he pattered along the edge making sure his foot stayed clear of the muddy side.

Dore village playground, known commonly as the 'Rec', was separated from the private facility by a skeletal thicket of hawthorn, itself disguising a downtrodden barbed wire fence. Absolutely no obstacle for Robbie who remembered quickly where the easiest gap sat - about eight yards along. Not having played this old game since the summer of 2004, he took a side-step climb, lifting the wire without difficulty.

(I did it - I managed it in the dark!) His excitement distracted him enough not to avoid the deep ditch underneath. Slipping with both feet as he turned, Robbie dropped straight through the trap-door of brambles. It wasn't a big deal though - while at least two feet in depth, he landed upright and uninjured.

(Oops, I'm clumsy. Should still leave laughing and that, till I'm out the other side.)
As he pulled his way back out along a nearby branch, he felt a hefty yank at the back of his head, before discovering his hat had gone. Looking back behind, he saw the thief was in fact a branch off a partially fallen tree above.

The hat hung like a bird feeder from one of the more depleted branches left in situ. Making back to grab it, Robbie heard movement, much closer. Loud rustling from the ditch, not far ahead put the wobbles up the boy. Movement also joined from within the gorsy vegetation. Quite possibly a squirrel or blackbird at first, the shape was too large and, clearly of more than two legs.

Robbie pictured the image of a fox emerging from the darkness, geared to maul him into shreds. Receding, terrified, he faced completely backwards, clambering through the remaining trees, monitoring whatever lurked in the overgrowth, until he fell sideways, landing through onto hard grassed floor.

Discovering he'd reached the 'Rec' side, he stood and listened to the continued rustling assuming whatever the creature was, was still on his trail. Robbie backed away slowly, finding himself in the enclosed children's playground area: quite handy right now, especially if he could place the swing between himself and the offending stalker. Reversing watchfully away from the trees, he kept alert to anything with eyes that might emerge this side.

"Come on..." he finally let it out loud "Try it mate. Come on - think you're hard enou..."

His childish threat was cut, as a huge lump-like object struck from behind, sending him flat to the ground. Thinking the creature bigger than first presumed, he lay there for a moment, resigned to being a goner before pulling himself cautiously up one final time to study whatever had come for him.

It was now that he met the large dark shape that looked over from about seven feet above. Almost still, bar a vague sway brought by the wind, a faint grey face gazed down on him its eyes totally darkened within their sockets.

(ii)

The blue VW Passat tore along the infinitely vibrant urban corridor that was Abbeydale Road and into the first - and hopefully *final* for the occupants - of its many dual carriageway segments.

"No, no, don't … please."

The female driver sighed as she watched the ocean of green lights ahead, praying that they didn't become yellow before she reached them. (*For Christ's sake, we're cops; we shouldn't have to put up with this.*) The double-file flow seemed totally impregnable, as Detective Inspector Joanne Leyton pinned her eyelids wide open in frustration.

"Told you we shouldn't have come out in an unmarked job." commented her younger male cohort on the passenger side.
"It looks like it's about to *have* some marks put on it...." she dismissively replied. "...oh, look."

A sizeable break in the traffic suddenly appeared like a long undiscovered well in someone's garden. Leyton played bongos with the wheel as she watched the chicane, amongst the cars closest in front and a *FirstBus* double-decker, widen vaguely to her favour. She carefully released the brakes as it dispersed, the black Honda Civic alongside breaking off left as the bus grumbled on ahead.

"Hold tight. And the Superintendent doesn't hear of this - not that you'd be horrid enough to grass me up anyway."

DC Garstone knew it would have been easier just to inform the team they'd be taking a few minutes extra getting up there.

"God, y'know something ma'am, I won't half be celebrating when we get our radios back again."

Leyton smirked aside, aching to respond, but had to delay whilst watching the lights like a trained eagle. (*Don't you dare, matey!*) The green turned to amber, she slammed on the accelerator and, with no oncomings about to cut up her trajectory, threw the VW violently right and upwards.

From here, she had to play on wild cards, finding the route towards the village. Asking Garstone for geographical info was futile, he'd been serving on the Sheffield team only six months longer, at a year and was still reduced to calling streets, he couldn't name by preposterously puerile descriptions. As she roared up *'that big hill with the trees'*, Leyton brought up the recent sad story of a few police radios and a fishpond. Acting like not listening, Garstone was occupied with straightening himself, almost hurled through the window by that frightening flying turn earlier - one of many techniques actually taught her by *him*.

"People usually do this sort of speed trying to get away from scenes like this, not when heading for them." he rolled out another of his natural witticisms.
"Yeah, heh," she duly humoured him, finding his Geordie accent made them more digestible "If my own laws applied in the world, we'd be afforded twice the rights of our uniformed brethren to flout the speed lim.... oohhh, close!"

Leyton applied both sets of brakes with a screech audible a mile away, as the top junction loomed. It was a miracle as to whether she actually noticed any vehicles approaching as she turned left onto the main road at the end, clearly another prominent trunk route out of town. Finding a quieter stretch of tarmac in front, she found time to chat.

"So, what's the story that brings us all the way to Dore then?"
"You sound like you know the place."
"Yes, one of Sheffield's top-rung 'toff troughs', I understand. Hardly the place for murders, you'd think: then again, I have been informed of other things destroying the village's tranquillity as badly."

"Aye, like…"
"Like the army of ducks outside the florists, I've been warned enjoy a walk or two across the road during the day."
"Well you said Dore's *'posh'*, like, but that…"
"Save it." she paused Garstone "Its time to go *'just that little bit faster'* again."

Re-entering urban scenery, she parped frantically, deterring anyone from reversing off their drives, before swooping down the street through an s-bend to yet another last-second brake assault. Easing off from the bollard-lined exit, her passenger was just sat thinking how events might have ended were a vehicle capped in turquoise blue lights travelling by right at this time, when his colleague brought him back to reality.

"Well, here's our ducks." Leyton pointed out as a trio of tiny white heads appeared in front of the bonnet. "Oh and by the way, my 'florists' actually happens to be a greengrocers, sorry."
"I think I could take one of these little fellas home with me, now you've mentioned it." Garstone joked.

He leant out of the window admiring the little web-footed creatures that paraded suicidally across the road in front.

"That might be possible soon, Greg, as in 'confiscated from their owners for obstructing a highway'. Now, are they going to save us the pain or …aw no-o-o-o-o!"

Garstone jumped out and walked round the side to discover one of the smaller ducks taking refuge under the front wheel. Rarely spotted out of the car without his ivory trench-coat, he was more than sorely tempted to smuggle one home right now, were it not for being on the way to a crime scene.

"C'mon little chap, best not break the Green Cross Code now."

Scooping the protesting bird up with both hands, he ferried it back to the verge where its friends were also now retiring, one by one.

"Excuse me *Dr Dolittle*," Leyton called across through the window "I think we'd better get moving."

Checking her mirror again, she'd just noticed a familiar Volvo Estate slowing up behind the delivery van.

"Well he's got an obstacle so we're safe... for about two minutes, "Garstone consoled as he jumped back into the seat.
"Right, I wouldn't really like to say this when it's us speeding," said Leyton, "but it's now a case of *'spot the flashing blue lights'*."

She loosened the clutch slowly and rolled away, allowing the grubby white van into its usual daily space. Praying it would obstruct the other car behind long enough, Leyton held the pedal until they reached forty again, only to suddenly find themselves almost taken out by a police unit coming in off a junction at left.

"Looks like we've just got blue *tape* to make do with."

The DI regarded reality once more as she was diverted towards a cordoned driveway on her right, chaotically over-laden with arrivals sporting 'SOUTH YORKSHIRE POLICE' along their bodywork. A fluorescent-suited officer stepped out to welcome them.

"Morning, ma'am." the young uniformed cop acknowledged "We were starting to get worried something had happened."
"Something will, if we don't get out of sight pretty quick."

Though pointless for a cop whose reputation preceded her, Leyton habitually flashed her ID before mooring up in the car park and rapidly disembarking, her inquisitive DC in tow. A sizeable party massed around the near end of the playground swings. Leyton recognised half of the faces all at once including that of DC Leroy Armitage, a man always enlightened by her presence.

This was small fry however, compared to what his current DI received from the other regular officers on her appearance. For some, Leyton's slender 5'10" frame accomplished the task itself but for the deeper minded her unmistakably prominent turn-out in burgundy trouser suit and tied-back mousy hair commanded discipline alone. Rarely seen without her black leather-bound clipboard tucked underarm, her more characteristic aspects turned heads for reasons she much preferred to those of the condescending type.

Detective Constable Greg Garstone was equal halves the same as he was different. Conspicuously younger at 26 he still had a substantial enough education to see her for what she was as a *police officer* as opposed to 'potential sex object', a shining example to most up to 20 years his senior. A formidably intelligent human within this outer shell, either way Leyton got him listening without question.

This said Garstone couldn't escape the feeling that his looks appealed to Leyton though. His youthful, chiselled face and short fair hair, always brushed flat spelled 'handsome hunk from out of fifth form' as well as fuelling her long-verified fondness of all men six feet-plus. She was often tempted to say so but was in fear of setting the wrong example.

A keen admirer of Leyton for all reasons, DC Armitage rose as usual on her approach. A moderately built mixed-race, also of

Leyton's age Armitage's persona was, in contrast the archetypal Yorkshire lad; his broad Sheffield dialect was also often a real handful to get round. While as tough an officer as the next, he had long been the resident joker of the pack although his boss did not seem in the mood for pleasantries today.

"Right, who have we got..." The DI intruded, squatting round the crowd, "Hmmm, someone who looks a little too old to be playing on swings."

Armitage revealed the heap slumped against the end bar. Lifting it over, Leyton found herself looking down on a middle-aged male of fairly shortish size, with dark straggly hair and bushy moustache that looked brown at one end dissolving to a neglected grey. The man's savagely depleted red sweater, one sleeve rolled up, the other almost totally down gave the impression that he'd closely escaped a bomb. His head, wearing a very white, slightly blue-ish face protruded through a mass of dark iron chains, circled a complete three times at least round the throat.

"Sorry you had to end it this way, '*Roy Ecclesby aged 41 of no57 St David's Rise, Abbeydale Road South, Sheffield.*'"

She perused an item from the man's wallet that lay on the floor right underneath him.

"Can't be suicide, this' Armitage quipped, "I don't think anyone on their own'd make that good a job of the chaining."
"The majority of dog-owners do put in a reasonable effort."
"Didn't make you out to be a *dog* person, ma'am." quipped Armitage.
"No, I'm more of a *cat* woman any day; but as you're duly volunteering," Leyton handed him another part of the chain "demonstrate kindly if you will, how you'd make your dad's faithful Gunter secure while in the supermarket."

14

Not quite sure - as always - what his boss was up to, Armitage passed it round the end post and, holding the fed end as tight as his fingers coped, dragged the piece three complete times round.

"Well, perhaps not you, but most do take the time. I just hope I'm never driving past that Co-op when you're around."

"Forgive me for interrupting your fun, DI Leyton," A gruff voice turned them away from their activities. "...but you might realise you have just involuntarily put your fetid paw mark on a murder item."

"Well, no disrespect, sir," Leyton boldly addressed the stony, haggard man in his mid-fifties who now hung his face right over hers "But seeing *as* there was no DNA left by the lovely chap who did this, at least someone has now compensated you. Satisfied?"

"Will be, the day you crawl back into that Wrangelford squirrel-hole you once slithered out of."

Leyton could only sigh as the typically blinkered Detective Chief Superintendent, Derek Hargreaves fired off his daily tirade.

"Well now you've finished playing 'chain the dog', are you going to talk to the witnesses before they also go walkies?"

"And where might *they* be?" She scanned round the gathering of cars and people, emptily understanding where he was pointing.

"Well there's only one but given that, I hoped you might have been under way. As usual you disappointed me by poking your nose in where you saw fit instead."

"Oh, alright, spare me the hot air act sir. I'll go and see to it." She swung her hand to summon Garstone, "Greg, come on, let's move before the *magic white tent* rises up."

"It's a magic white *stick* you need, you incompetent trollop!" Hargreaves snarled inaudibly, behind her.

Often bewildered by her affectionate term for the crime scene forensics tent, he felt a smidgen of indulgence in finally harbouring the basis to express a long-contained opinion.

His newly recruited DI, on the other hand had about fifty she was prepared to unleash in the face of Superintendent Hargreaves without any sense of guilt brought by the authority barrier between them. Her first six months of serving under this horribly chauvinistic man had been anything but lovely and at the bulk of times comparable to working in a prison labour camp.

The top brass within the South Yorkshire Constabulary had eagerly welcomed DI Leyton's transfer because of the remarkable wit and ingenuity she displayed within her previous post. Over thirteen years with the Cambridgeshire unit she'd worked for straight out of graduation, no one could fail to observe her level of perseverance for such a young officer, Leyton's by-the-book approach playing second fiddle to her swiftly acquired eye for detail.

A person looked up to by all who'd served alongside back in her idyllic southern surroundings; Leyton's unmistakable flair for initiative grated constantly with her current leader's my-way-or-the-doorway attribute and had made the pair firm enemies since the morning of April 27th, 2011. The feud had escalated since the end of summer with a dispute over a week's paid holiday which he'd decided (solely by his own authority) that she wasn't entitled to; it didn't show signs of reconciliation anytime soon.

Hargreaves was by no means making it personal. A born misogynist, he had a career-long belief that police work was strictly a man's world, dating right from his humble beginnings as a young graduate constable. All Leyton could do for the time being was keep her head down and maintain the undertaking of her duties to her continuously reputable standards.

Both Garstone and she were already nearly halfway down the ten-inch wide tragedy of mud and water that just vaguely resembled a path, and could see that the amount of police vehicles in the car park was beginning to exceed its meagre 8-berth capacity.

"I believe we have a witness," she blurted behind PC Jackson who had his back to her, obviously awaiting new arrivals.
"Aye, ma'am." the PC said, turning halfway round "I suppose you could call him one."
"Well old grumble-guts there did on appearing. Do you know where I might find the person in question?"
"You're just about looking right at him."

Jackson pointed into the clump of trees to her right. Leyton could just make out something in there that wasn't as green as its dominant surroundings.

"You won't get much out of him, I have to warn you: the only question he was capable of answering straight, was his first name."
"I think you'd better take the dive this time, ma'am," Garstone soon talked himself out of it "You've got that special touch with people, his type."
"Well, thanks Greg - it's always good to know I've got your encouragement"

(iii)

She broke away with audible sarcasm, negotiating the decorative boulders into the shady overgrowth. Sitting on a stump, amidst this tiny patch of woodland was a young man in his late teens. Clad in a blue fleece zip jacket and black jeans, he sat with his hands clasped together and head ducked down, seemingly not wanting to know too much about the world around him at this time. Only a rustle of brambles, disturbed by one of Leyton's stilettos, aroused the youth's attention.

"Hello there..." she eased in her common introduction. "are you okay?"
"Er...I'm...I think... I'm alright." the boy mumbled, lifting his head up a little further.
"Are you going to tell me your name?"
"Robbie."
"Hello Robbie. I'm DI Leyton."

He raised his face further, and then gradually fully, to address this smartly clad lady stood before him.

"That's a nice name. Are you a policeman too?"
"Well it's 'police officer' actually, these days but yes, we are, sort of. 'D' stands for *detective*. That's why I don't wear 'police' things, you see."
"So you're not going to arrest me? I'm not a criminal?"
"Of course you aren't."

He backed away a little bit from her, remaining pensive and fragile in voice.

"Please don't arrest me. I only saw it after it happened."
"I've just said I won't. Come on, what happened."
"I don't know. There was a man in the playground. He was on the swing." Robbie became very tense and unsettled about whatever it was, troubling him. "Someone's killed a man! Killed him with a chain! The man on the swing! He's dead!"
"Okay love, calm down. I've now got to ask you a few questions.

18

No need to feel uncomfortable - just try to tell me what you saw. Okay?"

"Right...I think I can...yes, I can."

"Good lad…. oh, I see you've volunteered at last have you?"

She praised Garstone's appearance as he rustled through in on their conversation.

"Aye," he diverted her towards the swings again "Leroy says there's something he wants you to look at."

"And he thought *your* pad was less worthy of his precious ink than mine, did he?"

She turned once more to Robbie. "Okay. Listen, this is DC Garstone. He's another detective, like me. I've got to go and see someone now, so he's going to talk to you instead. Don't worry. He's just as friendly as I am."

"Alright…yeah."

The youngster seemed less cagey about strangers following his conversation with Leyton. Seeing that she could trust Garstone with her new friend, she strolled back to where Armitage was keenly awaiting. Feeling like a ping-pong ball with all this backward and forwarding between parties, she hoped to herself that her other DC's latest find was worthy of such an awkwardly-timed plead for her return.

"I hope its something new that's popped up in the long five minutes since I was last stood here."

"Could call it new I suppose," He beckoned her to something below the swing. "Think you'd best have a look at this."

Leyton crouched slowly and let her friend point it out using his pen

"I *may* have seen it before..." She commented at the small

hieroglyph-like symbol that been scratched into the ground. "Perhaps everywhere, except a murder scene."

"What do you think it means?" Armitage re-expressed his last query. "A chevron penetrating a circle... proper weird, that."

"Well, at least that *'someone'*s etching skills don't quite level up with their chain-fitting." Leyton lifted her head away, inviting Armitage in to see. "If you look closely, you'll notice more."

The DC squatted closely enough to note that the circular part was repeated three times over itself, obviously to establish shape. The other element forming the bizarre inscription was a careless triangle, minus its bottom side, the tip hitting right in the middle of the circle.

"S-o-o-o-o-o...." Leyton came back with the usual two-letter word, (that for her was a copyright-protected catchphrase) "While I'm not about to accuse Tutankhamen, it's easily the same individual who's hung poor Mr Ecclesby out to dry."

"And how do you work that out without the DNA samples, you little smart-arse?" The ever-present Superintendent Hargreaves had to throw his weight in once again.

"Well then," she began, showing him the end of the chain "What else do we know to make as deep a scratch?"

To prove a point, she dug a short line on the floor using the severed link, creating a gouge about one-and-a-half millimetres deep - as severely cut in as the 'hieroglyph' itself.

"Looks like you're right... unfortunately." He examined the result as Leyton matched them. "Right, boys," he declared, with his typical absence of gratitude, "Goldilocks here has succeeded in blowing her trumpet again, so pack up, unless you're stopping for the other fun."

As they all diverged for their respective vehicles or other various duties awaiting them en route, Garstone stood waiting about halfway along the path for Leyton, clutching a plastic pink/yellow wallet.

"Found some treasure in the trees have we?" she seemed impressed for once today.
"Turns out his name's Robbie Draycott. Special Needs student, according to this pretty-coloured little card."
"So much for the soft touch, I mean, *who* authorised you to demand his identity, exactly." (*There IS a difference between a witness and a suspect*)
"Keep your voice down." he gestured discreetly over his shoulder at Hargreaves. "T'was *he.*" His announcement drew a gasp of total abhorrence from Leyton "Hey, I noticed Robbie's got issues 'up there' but at least he cooperates. Should fix the Super' up with a few lessons."

His DI enjoyed the continuation of Garstone's comedy routine this morning, though still had to cut short the laughter, in concern over where Robbie had disappeared. Garstone answered that before it had even been asked, something he was more than very good at with Leyton.

"The boys are looking after him."
"Poor them." the ever-present Hargreaves eavesdropped.
"Someone's got to, sir." Garstone bravely answered back.
"All the more reason you should have pulled him, Garstone," the Superintendent ranted, indignantly, "so why not either take the opportunity, or drop him back at his mummy's?"
"I actually think that'll be what the boy prefers," Leyton made a beeline for Robbie, whom she'd spotted still mounted on his woodland perch.
"And having done that, drop yourself off too; preferably somewhere out of my sight."
"Likewise."

She glanced halfway back at him as they strode into Robbie's 'lair'. DCS Hargreaves was old at fifty-four but far from deaf, and far less stupid than he sounded. Robbie, still not exactly numb to the world either saw the Superintendent gloating in his direction. He leapt up in a panic, making to run till Garstone blocked him."

"What's he said about me?" Robbie gabbled "Am I in trouble?"
"No, course not" Garstone soothed him "Don't worry about Superintendent Hargreaves, he's an idiot. Come along now - we're gonna take you home."
"Do you think it's best to let *him* set off first," Leyton advised "hoping that we'll get separated somewhere along the way?"

Garstone nodded in near-confined agreement as they watched Hargreaves climb into his car, ignoring everyone around him. Robbie leapt into the back of Leyton's carriage and thrust his seat belt on, every bit as eager to leave, though endlessly inquisitive.

"Is he horrible to everyone, all the time?"
"You got it mate." Garstone smiled then whispered indiscreetly to Leyton.
"Hey, look - if the kid knows to belt up like, you know he's going to be an easy ride."

Leyton, not listening, reversed the car round like something from the movies and made for the gateway. Seemingly a little more relaxed in manner, she took her time in looking both directions, before turning back out onto Townhead Road. Not that she a lot of choice with Armitage's red Ford Focus sat right in front of her, she could make out the glowing rear light of the Superintendent's car, disappearing right, at the junction ahead.

"Enemy retreating," she sighed. "Come on, Leroy old boy, make

my day."

Armitage's car finally rolled off and hers took its turn. Just as soon though, the little scarlet hatchback slammed on its brakes again. A brightly-clad form shot past in front of him.

"Ah... well there's another one who could be of help."
She leant over to the left across Garstone, who was getting used to it this morning.
"Hold on, where did he g...*oh NO-O-O!*"

2

THE SPARROW LAY SNARED

(i)

For all his troubles, young Danny Bennington was no stranger to cycle accidents- he had only departed his BMX saddle a fortnight before at Twentywell stunt track but this one really seemed to have put the wind through him. Probably because it involved dodging an oncoming cop car, rather than a concealed puddle this time, that he had just reason to be shaken. It did not help to find a stockily built Afro-Caribbean man lunge straight from a car door at him waving Danny's least favourite object, a Police ID. No fool when becoming confronted by any representative of the law, let alone DC Armitage, he revolved quickly to flee. Snatching his bike from the floor, however a second obstacle, much more fearsome appeared: the slim but commanding shape of DI Leyton.

"I ain't done nothin'!" he protested, petrified.
"I'm sure you haven't, Danny," she seemed pleased to see him again, "Though I can't help commenting on how prematurely that ASBO banning you from the Rec has expired."
"I weren't going in there, I swear." the teenager pleaded.
"He has a point, ma'am." Garstone rescued him "I can't see him trying that sort of stunt, with about 35 uniform there mulling over a murder. Though, if Superintendent Hargreaves had had his way…"
"Aw shit, not him!"

Danny pivoted on the utterance of that ghastly name, making to leap off across the kerb, only for Armitage to pin him in half-nelson.

"Have it your way then...." she said then turned to Garstone "Greg you and I'll take *trouble* and his two-wheeled machine back to 'base': Leroy can meanwhile drop Robbie back to more comfortable surroundings, i.e. his *house*."
"Straight home? What if the Super..."
"...*finds out?* You can tell him I ordered you to do it. Oh and in case you... forget, I just have. Okay guys let's roll."
"Heh, okay ma'am." Garstone handcuffed Danny, placing him in the back seat of Leyton's wagon in exchange for their more legitimate passenger.

The swish powder-blue paint scheme which the interview rooms of Midelson Road HQ had been treated to over the summer, was intended for a more relaxing feel than the rank off-white of earlier times. Unlike seasoned suspects, Danny Bennington barely noticed, sitting with his legs sprawled wide either side of the chair whilst readying his defiant backchat lines for later. The discomfort of finding himself sat in a room across a table from the watchful glare of two police officers did little to trouble Danny, by far a not unfamiliar situation for him.

One - DC Garstone; this friendly young lad-next-door type, prepared to play the friendly copper simply wanting a chat on a completely *innocent-till-proven-guilty* basis. He was in favour of offering a nice easy ride to a kid he hated to see in trouble, even if it hadn't been the first time they'd crossed paths these last months. The second - of course embodying the domineering DCS Hargreaves, purely opted to be the bad cop partnering the good. Declining to reserve even the merest compassion for anyone on the opposite side of the table, he shook his head in resentment at his subordinate's molly-coddling techniques.

"Why don't you just tell us why you chose the scenic route to the

25

newsagents today?”

Garstone still found room for patience with Bennington after over thirty minutes.

“It'd be a lot easier, then we can all go home… right sir?”

“Not if I have my way.” Hargreaves slammed a dampener on things as he always did. “I enjoy having him inside the station's secure confines as opposed to out, darkening Sheffield's doorways.”

“I think that's a bit harsh, sir. Danny's a good kid, just gets in with the bad crowd. My young brother…”

“*Was just the same, blah-de-bloody-blah-blah.* Pack up the soft touch, son, I know his type.”

(Once a yob, always a yob - makes no difference what turns him into one, let alone what turns him out of it again,) Hargreaves shook his head apathetically, nudging Garstone with the proverb implying his non-belief in reform; the only change this man ever recognised was the sort that he got from picking up the morning paper. He gloated frostily at Danny to ensure he most importantly understood that too, snatching the pencil off him and treading it into the floor.

“Now, Bennington, are you going to answer us, so that you stand a likelihood of going home tonight?”

“Hard as it is saying this, Dan, he's kind of right actually.” Garstone had to assert his own persuasions at last “Come on, mate, you're keeping yourself here as long as us.”

“I told you before - I get a lawyer, I'll talk.”

Danny was not uneducated enough to keep him from knowing his own rights, not that the superintendent believed he had any.

“So you think they'll come galloping all the way to bail out self-righteous little toe-rags they hear snivelling about *the big nasty old bobby,* eh?” Hargreaves mocked him, “Face it, my son, you‘d

26

even make a pea look clever."

"Thought I were entitled to one, that's all."

"He's got a point, sir." Garstone retrieved the courage to negate his numero uno "We have detained Danny without reading him his rights; that is something to consider."

"You love switching sides don't you, Garstone." Hargreaves smelt a frequently re-appearing rat here.

"Hey mate, you not spoke to Robbie the Retard yet?" suggested Danny, "He were around at the time it went off."

Not as stringent on the constraints of political correctness as Leyton, Garstone still found it hard not to flinch at such a strongly blunt remark, one that probably passed right over Hargreaves's head. Still he kept his opinion bottled, substituting a merely firmer tone as he continued with Bennington.

"If you are on about a chap called Robbie Draycott, yes we have already met today. DI Leyton took a statement from him at the scene."

"Hey, if you bring that bird in, I'll talk to *her*, ok."

"The 'bird' - Detective Inspector Leyton as she might actually prefer being called- is, as I told you, out at the moment, but she'll be back soon."

"Which means," began Hargreaves, "that without your Auntie Leyton round to play favourites, you can talk to *us* - if you know what's good for you that is."

Getting only silence once again, he shoved his face so far into Danny's that his Bronson-like moustache tickled against the kid's blemish-ridden nose.

"So go on then...." The Superintendent jabbed his biro into Danny's chest, "Why don't we play while waiting?"

"Playin' favourites you mean?" Danny still felt fearless of retaliation "You pigs like a bit of that - how come you ain't the

bottle right here?"
"Button it, you little tw… Oh, decided to drop yourself back here instead have you?"

He sensed a further presence with the creak of the door, and angrily revolved to find his favourite woman had been listening. The Superintendent walked off, dragging the door recklessly shut behind him.

"Just as well, it seems," Leyton persevered what might have just been about to happen. "Righty-ho, Danny, it's back to civilisation."
"Hiya." the boy practically leapt to his feet to welcome her.
"Er, Dan would you excuse us for a minute?" Garstone ushered her outside.
"I assume you got something out of him, with Hargreaves the Horrible's assistance." she acknowledged.

Leyton always probed him for an instant justification over being whisked out from the interview room, even in the politest of ways. Garstone allowed for a passing breath before answering but it seemed she wasn't one for delay this evening.

"No, just the usual thing; gave us the silence treatment for half an hour solid, until promised a solicitor at his side. Would've got more but with the Guv being ther…"
"Don't worry, that's about right for Danny."
"Said you and he go back a bit, plus he seems to know 'Robbie the Retard'… er, as he calls him."

Mentally challenged' was obviously seen to use too much spit for Danny, but Leyton found it quite acceptable in front of Hargreaves, a man so little at risk of being shocked, given his everyday attitude to anyone fitting such category as Robbie Draycott's was about identical to Danny's at the best of occasions.

"Moving onto points more relevant, what's he actually said?"
"Not much, apart from *almost* owning up to bumping Mr Ecclesby off."
"You'd better hope he was joking!"
"He demands a lawyer, that's all so far."
"Hasn't it occurred to you we're actually supposed to be at the mortuary, identifying a body... either that or making small talk with the knowing Dore public?" Leyton retracted with tension "All Danny's doing is just trying to find out if being a murder suspect will make him look good."

She needed to judge Danny's coin by its double flip side, best understanding the two particularly common forms of suspect demeanour during interrogation. The other typical class, absent here was the one who stuttered their lines more frequently as the interview progressed: constantly assaulting a lone pencil on the table till it was almost in two halves while all the time foraging every explanation that hadn't a chance in hell of fooling the law.

Danny had breached an Anti Social Behaviour Order, if attempting to pass within the Rec but this remained an unsafe case; no witnesses had come forward to report him loitering thereabouts. Though legally a grey area, Danny didn't keep himself in its lighter shade through the torrent of impertinence displayed to Garstone and Hargreaves all afternoon - in fact, out of a carefree rebel like him, it spelt *'I did it'* to most police worth their salt.

(The murderer often visits the scene of his crime), that ancient chestnut dropped on Leyton again - *the classic passer-by act put to practice*. Danny had been literally just that, caught sauntering his merry way down Townhead Road. By testimony of the two other officers watching, he'd made no even slight attempt to pass

into the exclusion zone; his focus attached to another destination altogether. Ultimately, this lad had a line he wasn't quite made for crossing. Leyton read it from the last time he'd been hauled in at the desk, vandalism and spitting being the worst of his offences, plus the occasional truancy notice but violent crimes were still a strain on his limitations. Garstone felt that on his patience by now. Executive decisions from DI Leyton weren't often going to come without another study of the detainee.

"We decided on his fate then?" Garstone came back with the question he was aching badly to ask.
"Beg your pardon?"
"Super wants the kid booked, preferably for the murder."
"Hey, freeze right there, fly-boy!" Leyton put up both her hands to halt him. "No one's said anything about Danny being a killer."

Despite having been on the team only half as long as he had, she read her boss's less than by-the-book tactics without even lifting the cover, so had reason to be appalled at her DC's cavalier attitude. Never in a month of Sundays did she condone the act of booking someone for the sake of it. Harder for her still, Hargreaves very seldom let anyone leave his station un-charged, Bennington's capture having earned him a timely excuse to wreak his long suppressed vengeance on the kid's social class. Virtually leaping at any slight possibility of a collar, the first day on a major case, the privilege to bang 'Chav scum' like Bennington up forever was one not to be sniffed at. Judge, jury and jailer, having dealt with Danny's type all his working life the key he swung needed to thrown away before it became worn.

"Nothing's happening to him then?" Garstone wouldn't ever go without a straight *yes* or *no* but she specialised in riddles. "Just walking out of here, like that?"
"Greg, between prints and props, there was nothing to find at the scene other than that thing carved into the earth. The bizarrely

tidy nature of this murder - let alone a total absence of DNA - makes it infinitely hard to match: with Danny or anyone's."

"Don't wish to sound like I'm arguing, ma'am but we're down to two options - holding Danny one more night in case the kid coughs up anything relevant, or letting him go with a firm few words regarding wasting police time."

Garstone slowly swung his head both ways, prompting his boss to finalise on where Bennington's evening might end. She started to perform her 'thinking' walk down the corridor then whirled round again.

"Well I know which one is destined to piss off Hargreaves off, the most."

"Sure do." he chortled, opening the door. "Okay kid, time for the wide world again."

"Eh? You're kiddin'…. that it?" Danny immediately got cocky.

"Just remember who's back we're going behind, here."

Obviously not likely to get a 'thank you' from him any more than from Hargreaves, Leyton marched Danny to the front desk and let him sign himself out. He finally replied, on putting the pen down.

"Where's me bike then? You keeping it or something?"

"No, it's a bit too small for me, wouldn't you think? Actually, Greg on the subject…" she clawed Garstone back in, thrusting him her keys "can you do the honours - you live close enough to his neck of the woods."

"Gleadless?" Garstone chortled in amazement at her geographical inaccuracy "That's getting on for about three miles away!"

"Don't worry; you will be the one laughing loudest when it shows on Hargreaves's petrol expenses."

31

Garstone escorted Danny to the parked Vauxhall Vectra, shaking his head at how far she seemed prepared to return her spite against the Superintendent. Leyton backed from the door and drew her mobile, her sidekick's hunch prompting her to try Robbie's parents again. Then as she was halfway searching through her list of long, pretty numbers, something occurred to her: she'd forgotten to get it off Armitage, who was long on his way home by now.

Her only hope was to try Garstone's desk. Making straight for the office, she marched hurriedly through the door, doing a beeline for the desk third at left. (*Greg had taken over the controls from me when I was called back to examine Mr Ecclesby again*) she thought. (*He's bound to have it jotted.*)

"Something keeping you here, Leyton?" a gruff and familiarly unpleasant Yorkshireman's voice rang across from the back of the office, like an old ghost in the corner.
"I was just wondering if it was likely that Greg would have acquired a phone number from Robbie."
"Don't kid yourself, duckie, what makes you think he's going to let *you* run wild with it? I thought his mum and dad might have done you the service when you let them have him back tonight. (*Then again, they might have done the sensible thing and gone ex-directory, once they saw you coming.*)"
"I wasn't actually the officer who drove Mr Draycott home, but it's among the usual avenues I try."
"Well try it elsewhere, I've got a home to get to- and you know I'm hardly going to trust you in here alone."

Hargreaves clicked his fingers and signalled her towards the door, establishing that there was no chance of leeway in the matter.

"And that means no going knocking on any people's doors. I'd hate to be the butt of complaints about you inflicting your Cambridge-bred cakehole on the public any more than can already be helped."

"It's called 'initiative' sir; it does move things along a bit in a murder case."

"It's called *sticking your nose about*, in your case. If you want to talk, it goes through me through me. New rule I'm making with you, Leyton. Not having you try your freestyle tactics out for size in here, understood?"

His DI screwed a face at him as he turned to lock, before marching away though she remained proudly adamant of owning the higher ground.

Realising that he was following her right out of the building, Leyton hastened her pace right up to the Passat. On looking back round, to see Hargreaves had stopped to talk to Sgt Daniels outside the main doors, she eased herself into the seat and tried the phone again, praying that Armitage had his hands-free switched on, if not Garstone.

(ii)

The call attempt again unsuccessful, plus so almost caught by Hargreaves, Leyton eased her Passat out of the gateway hoping not to see, or be seen by *him* for as long as the day remained. Yet it seemed hard even now as the glow of more headlights - a Volvo 540 - filled her wing mirror.

Coming to the crossroads outside, Hargreaves's car closely tailed her, as if attached by a tow rope.

As she stopped to give way, Leyton saw through the glare to the shape behind the dashboard. Immense and domineering, the Superintendent's moustache just began to show above his scornful pout, with absolutely no iota of tact or compassion readable on that face made of hard nosed spite. His feelings towards her were little friendlier on the road than in the office.

The 'tache was joined by two dark tunnelly eyes as he poked his full face forward, lifting his window mirror to communicate - he did this with a small tipping of his finger, pointing ahead the road which was now clear. Anxious he'd be due to succeed it with a few choice words through her window, Leyton threw her other paranoid cautions to the wind and pulled away.

Trying to lose him at every possible roundabout between Mosborough and Handsworth, they eventually split on reaching the parkway. On getting into the city again, she looked over her seat at the rear window as it re-filled itself with ivory light at the colossal roundabout. Turing out to be a black Ford Mondeo behind her, she acknowledged the riddance of her nemesis with scheming satisfaction.

(I'll show him who says I can't visit who I wish when off duty.)

She remembered the Draycott's address, chanting it to herself.
(17 Highcroft Grove ... 17 Highcroft Grove)
Setting her course for Abbeydale Road, it didn't take her more than a minute to forget. Pulling aside, almost into a bus lane, she slipped her memo pad out.
(No 17... Oops-s s it was 'CLOSE', not 'Grove'.)
Keeping the page, she bent the pad as far back as its stiff leather cover could take then wedged it underneath her handbrake, before returning to the road.

Predicting Hargreaves was long on the way home to his Pitsmoor semi, if not there by now the aura of lamps painting out the street

34

in their nightly amber turned many vehicles into a darkish grey-green colour, which meant anybody could be still behind her.

No need to worry unless it says 'Volvo' she thought before she forced it out of her mind.

A further set of lights, familiar to her showed through the trees ahead, those being the beacons of Beauchief crossroads. Without a murder call to answer this time, Leyton allowed for the reds, though made it through clean on ambers. The rush hour long over, she gave herself all the time she wanted to turn up the hill: the route to Dore traced itself from here on. Being the DI's second trip this way rather than her first, paid dividends to her navigation in the dark including that junction at the top.

Stopping for the sole passing car at the top of the climb again, the lights of a Vauxhall Vectra bearing in from the right froze her solid. Hargreaves was one problem, but her over-protective DC also getting wind of her extra curricular liaisons was a tight second. As the Vauxhall driver slowed to gift her right of way, Leyton just looked to the left and slowly pushed away, taking her time to avoid suspicion.

(It won't be him, why would Greg be back up here?)

She aimed off down Limb Lane, ignoring whoever it had been. Another four minutes trying to alleviate herself of these worries took her almost right past her stopping point. Heading up Townhead Road, she just saw the left hand turn she needed at the last second.

Caught up by the sharp left onto Highcroft Close, Leyton hastily went wrong-side to negotiate the turn, but at least it rescued her concentration from the jaws. A direct separation of houses on one side and hedges the other; the darkness instantly   misguided her into thinking *'shit - wrong road'* as she rolled along to the end.

(17…17… Come on)… She counted the doors along till the address stopped beside.

Finding a space *just* big enough to park, Leyton made sure she'd be able to get out again later, then leapt out and along to the house she remembered rightly was No17.
Light from a front room window enabled the two brass-plated digits to glint, guiding her right to the correct gate.

As she pushed the creaky wrought-iron gate open, Leyton just missed tripping on an erratically placed brick, clearly meant as the wedge. She stopped to move it aside, lest it caught her on her departure. The activity drew a figure to the window. As Leyton smiled, the woman that had opened her curtain to check on the intruder eyed her frostily and turned away.

Charming, thought Leyton stepping briskly down the drive and pressing the bell.
(I'd better do things properly before I upset them even more.)

Stood as smartly as she always did, Leyton allowed for the occupant to reach the door in her own time. About half a dozen different locks slid back before the door finally opened.

"And what might *you* be wanting?" demanded the face peering from the murky kitchen light behind.

Barbara Draycott, a lady of moderate stature, in her late fifties, eyed Leyton up and down with a face of dislike. Leant against the doorway in her green/ brown cardigan, she definitely wasn't looking to welcome her in.

"I was hoping I'd be left alone for the day now."

"My apologies." Leyton showed her ID and introduced herself, without trying to justify her appearance as yet.

"I already guessed," Barbara dismissed the gesture, "You certainly have some nerve round on a visit at all today, let alone this hour. Now, can you kindly tell me your business or disappear?"

"Just a caring police officer making sure a star witness is ok. I am particularly concerned about your son Robbie following today's events.

"By that, you do imply that caring, concerned police officers routinely leave a mentally disadvantaged witness alone in the trees, ordering him to *shut the 'eff' up* - correct, DI Leyton?"

Barbara became visibly agitated by having to repeat her opinion on the police's treatment of Robbie today, to a further officer.

"Is that what you do now?! Throw people like him out of the way like some interfering random nobody!?"

"Probably not me. Very probably though: my so-called superior, DCS Hargreaves. I must tell you for the record, Mrs Draycott, that I am no fan of my boss's '2011BC' approach to police practice."

"I do recall him mentioning a man. Is this your *Hargreaves* friend?"

"Certainly no friend of mine," she almost laughed, and it finally rubbed off on Barbara who now disconnected her elbow from the doorway, stood more causally.

"I can't stand the man. I'd be still in Cambridge if I'd had my way...or *he'd* have his too."

As Leyton's feature length apology seemed to be some way off ending, Barbara sounded ready to hear the rest of it inside, rather than on her doorstep. She stood aside and showed her visitor in.

(iii)

"You're not about to sit down to dinner, are you?" Leyton made sure to sound considerate. "I could always leave it till tomorrow." "Well obviously, but now that you've travelled right from Midelson Road for the trouble..." Barbara directed her into the living room. "Have any seat you like. The kettle only takes two minutes."
"Thankyou."

Leyton took her place in one of the single armchairs, swapping a silent *Hi* with the small Japanese doll eyeing her from the dresser. Perched on the corner of the red silken seat in her trademark way, the detective gave herself item to take in the room, tidy and classy with little evidence of any male occupant. She lifted a magazine aside from the little table in front, clearing a mat for the cup to land on. Peering at *Railworld - (August 2011)*, which she could only assume was Robbie's, she found it an interesting read for about half a page in, before the rattling of spoons turned her head upwards to find her brew already arriving. Barbara lowered it onto the mat and smiled at Leyton, seemingly not objecting to her reading her son's own magazines without asking permission first.

"I couldn't help notice that you are also from the south somewhere, DI Leyton." she began her conversation again, randomly "Is that right?"
"'*Jo*', please. Yes, I transferred from Cambridgeshire early this year. Born and bred next to a university. Handy, don't you think?"
"Yes, it'd have certainly paid better than a life and career in Broadstairs."
"Oh, you shouldn't be that harsh. I holidayed there with my family when I was seven." Leyton pretended to dissuade her

modesty, "Then you grow up, I suppose."

"Yes, and go on to marry a Yorkshireman…" Barbara laughed.

Leyton took a sup of her new friend's well-concocted coffee and slowly lowered it. Something then had her immediately lift it away again. Barbara smiled again. She was glad one person wasn't committing her son's favourite crime of not using a mat - a habit that had contributed many an irremovable ring to her expensive marble - but couldn't help turning it to an intrigued stare, noticing Leyton's fascination with the coaster.

"Oh, do beg my pardon." Leyton slid another coaster over, to explain, "I just couldn't help but notice the pattern."

"No problem at all. Robbie made those."

"Really? They're lovely." She admired the brightly coloured abstract designs, each with its own scheme. "How old was he when he did these?"

"About a year younger than he is now, believe it or not. He made them at a ceramic arts café in Banner Cross. Rather useful when stuck for his mum's Christmas present, don't you think?"

Leyton got a quick grin in before another visit to the mug commanded her; then the serious issue of her visit set in once more and by now, there wasn't another friendly topic left to delay it with.

"Barbara, I don't wish to sound insensitive in any way here…." She still tried to look light-faced as she asked "but till now, I've had reason to understand that your son had suffered his disability as from birth. Is this not actually right?" She saw the smile plunge from Barbara's mouth. "I'm sorry."

"No, please, I don't mind, really." She put her cup down and shut the lounge door. "He was normal until he was thirteen… as best I can word it. "

"Thirteen - really that recent?"

"Normal for thirteen years longer than the idiots who did it, not that my Rob was supposed to have sat there and let them take advantage."
"Did what?"

Barbara knew that to move further along without crying she needed a strong sip of her still-boiling brew. She let Leyton wait, and then added.

"Do you know what an 'over -the- topper' is, Jo?"
"Other than the frequent consequence of flushing a blocked toilet, I can't say I do."
"He was on a swing. Robbie loved the Rec, when he was little. It was something he never outgrew, right till the end."

She laughed briefly one last time - this, for Leyton was her indication that the countdown to the sadder instalment was ticking. As Barbara looked at the floor, amassing her thoughts once more, she got ready for the darker depths of the tale.

"The end of...." Leyton gave it a push.

"Saturday morning, that July - the Summer Scout Gala was happening in the afternoon. Rob liked going up there to watch people setting up the stalls. They always looked out for him. He even took his bike up there but I banned him from doing after he nearly came off it into the candyfloss stand. Hence his resignation to life on the swings."
"And that's when it happened? Did someone attack him?"
"He loved going high on them - did't we all, when we were young? The goal he forever strove to achieve was an ov... you know, that thing I just told you."
"*Over-the-topper*...God...."

Leyton began to re-shape together what the term referred to.

"A couple of lads propping up the ropeway ride came across, probably couldn't help but ask Robbie why he was almost fetching it off the frame. Robbie just came out on the spot with it. He was bad enough at answering tings randomly in his normal days."

"So they pushed his swing a bit harder than he was used to?" Leyton felt it coming but was still confused as to how a 13 year old boy could still achieve such a feat, or not quite, as it seemed. "This is what made him fall off, I assume?"

(Their friend's parent owned a Land Rover, parked close by. It had a powerful petrol-driven winch attached to the back, capable of winding in the rope at up to 30mph. The two boys fixed hook end onto the back of Rob's swing, feeding it under the seat. Starting up the motor, they counted in unison, down from ten then pushed the button.)

"Oh, no…." Leyton nearly shrank from hearing the rest.

(Robbie almost cleared it, completing a full 180 degrees over before the chain then sagged from an abrupt loss of momentum. He was turning back upright already, this flip going into a quaver-like style. Robbie came down head first, sideways onto the crossbar before bouncing off to land on the floor, another seven feet below.)

"That's where the injuries were worst. He concussed his neck and left jaw on impact with the bar. Landing back on the floor was where most of the damage came from. Multiple haemorrhages and severe fracturing to the rear skull were amongst the worst." She looked down again, then up again at Leyton. "I hope I haven't given you nightmares."
"I shouldn't think so. I just work for one."

The humour went almost right over Barbara's' head as she sunk down, visibly close to crying.

"You should try the seven year nightmare *I've* lived, Jo; you don't know what it's like to live with a human jelly of a 20-year-old son for the rest of your day."
Her voice became raised and angrier. "It's like being caged with a dying animal you can't save! Excuse my rant, it just all becomes too much to be reminded of at times."
"How does your husband cope? Does he know what it's like?"
"Robbie's the reason Brian left. He didn't even want to find out."

Barbara reached a framed family picture down for Leyton, as she told her this, showing a 12-year-old Robbie in happier times.

"The constant screaming, the getting out of bed at five o 'clock in the morning to help him to the toilet… as if the three months in hospital wasn't bad enough to bear."
"That's rather disappointing. I thought an understanding father would be there for his child."
"Brian wouldn't understand water if he was pushed into the sea. He both loves me and our boy to bits but as long as Robbie stays under this roof, he vows to stay under another, far away as possible. The man simply couldn't find it in him to adapt. His father was little better, one of those Neanderthal working class types - always talked about 'weird' people as if they should be locked up."

Leyton took the photo for a quick look.

"He doesn't appear the uncaring kind." she said.

Looking at the smiling 48-year-old in a blue Fred Perry top behind his so-called beloved son, it was hard to believe how things were actually so different behind closed doors.

"He does have his moments, just they don't quite extend to his son almost dying, landing on his head from thirteen feet because of some small-brained adolescents who should have known better."
"Oh yes, by the way, did you follow up any charges against the youths responsible?"
"I told Brian to look into it. Sadly they'd already asked him, to which he simply replied 'No'. In other words, Jo, his one and only lad wasn't worth the hassle."
"What was there to stop you getting in contact with the police yourself?"

Leyton didn't know why but all of a sudden she became suspicious of Barbara.

"If Robbie hadn't survived, there could have been possible manslaughter charges."
"Brian asked me to keep quiet at the time. He was confident he would recover through completely. Obviously he regrets his anticipations now... as does his wife."

Leyton paid small attention to her slight pauses. Troubled by the subject, Barbara obviously needed to think about certain answers before giving them, though Leyton still couldn't conclude either way on the watertight realness of her sob story either way. Over the last half hour she had learned, to full devastating extent how Robbie's situation had proceeded to tear the household in two. Still, Leyton had to look at it on both sides of the coin, even if it didn't necessitate questioning Barbara more intrusively just yet.

Opting to invent her own excuses for the moment, Leyton placed the almost empty cup down, taking a final look at the coaster picture. Dodging Barbara's next likely line, she used them for a quick choice of subject change.

"I could do with a few of these for our office."

She tried to look as if she couldn't take her eyes off Robbie's impressive craftsmanship, although her interest in them was already showing as half-genuine.

"How many did he make?"
"Five, the other three are buried somewhere. He's also made a couple of larger ones since."
"That would be handy."

Leyton put her mug down on the one she'd gazed at all evening and stood, collecting her folder (brought with her rather unnecessarily it appeared).

"He keeps the bigger ones up in his room. Would you like him to show them?"
"Oh no, I'd better not disturb him."
"Please, it's a shame you've got to be on your way so abruptly."
"We'll meet again very soon." Leyton comforted her, "I'd rather Robbie didn't see me here tonight - he might be wondering who else I've got parked outside."
"Well, it's been nice meeting you, Jo." She showed Leyton out, "I certainly hope your Superintendent-cum-*non-friend* isn't out by the gate."
"I'm sure not."

Leyton quickly joked, abating the panic nearly begun through another mention of Satan's Superintendent. Feeling best that she adhered to her normal police protocols, if not to remain merely genuine, she passed Barbara one of her cards.

"Please don't hesitate to call if Robbie or you have problems.

Using this number will guarantee you'll find me on the line, and *not* DCS Hargreaves."

"Thankyou. You're a lot more understanding in comparison to your boss." Barbara's gratitude sounded vaguely emotional again. "I'll let you get off anyway. Can you see the gate alright in the dark?"

"I did when I came in through it...."

Leyton pretended to forget about the brick earlier as she strode back up to the Passat. Her own shifty posture almost leaked itself to Barbara, though the same would easily apply vice versa. She strongly latched onto the premonition that Robbie's mother had something to hide. Causing someone a crippling injury through reckless behaviour would be regarded as tantamount to an offence of GBH, so Barbara's reluctance to inform the police of his accident was primarily illicit.

She knew the law, including the parts of it below her enforcement. Looking back at the house, Barbara wasn't watching from the window this time. Leyton had won the trust of another member of public, though her victory for the day still seemed part empty.

Catching only six hours sleep was luxury enough for most people in this job, but for DI Leyton it housed a counterproductive taint. Waking up at half past five in the morning meant a whole two-and-a-half hours wait to find out what another day in the ever-sufferable world of the South Yorkshire Police force - and also of course DCS Hargreaves - was set to throw at her.

Her bowl of Kellogg's All Bran served as an unwelcome countdown clock in this case, each spoonful clocking another ten-fifteen seconds by, before time to step out of the door and set her beloved VW's trajectory for Midelson Road police station struck again. Nearly forgetting that she'd run the kettle, Leyton took the opportunity as she interrupted consumption of her cereal to pinch a look down at the streets of Sheffield city, the outside world that she seemed restricted to enjoy from her solitary 2nd floor window.

Returning to her seat, the All Bran was only about three-four good spoonfuls away from unveiling an empty bowl to the world once more, so in a strive to kill the time effectively up till 'lift-off', she swiped the box off the worktop and loaded the dish back up to spilling point.

It seemed in danger of failing today, as within another ten minutes the bowl was seven-eighths empty again, so she began picking the strands one by one with her fingers. Unsuccessful in filling up every useable moment up to half-past seven with the fast eater she was, there was only one last option.

Unbelievably, even to herself, she'd totally forgot to collect the Draycott's all evening she was there. Chancing back on a last-ditch strive to trace Robbie Draycott's phone number before she departed home for the day's duties, provided her with an opportunity to disturb Garstone.

Having got off on the wrong foot with Hargreaves again yesterday, a brief morning natter with the man she however hit it off with most, would ease her into that world across more of a smoother plain. Keying in the number, she quickly bolted another heaped spoon of All Bran and waited as the dialling tone began at the distant end.

"Come on Greggie boy, don't tell me you're still under the sh…"
"Oh, you've finally bothered to switch on, have you," a voice cut in at the other end.
"Yes as I'm on the hunt for Robbie's phone number, on the hint that you might have taken it yesterday."

"No…Aw no - you saying when Leroy took him home, he for..."

"Forgot to, *yes*…. Oops!"

"I'll call round later for it today if you like, not that we might have time."

"Oh, I see, got plans for us, have you?"

"Not involving a date, you'll be glad to know. He says to get up Green Oak Park in Totley, half-seven sharps. Apparently you'll never guess what's happened."

"No, and if '*he*' means Hargreaves, he'll get us when we bloody arrive. Listen, go straight there, Greg - if you detour to collect me, you'll be lucky to make *half ten*."

Switching off her phone and placing it on the table with her jacket, Leyton took one last look at the still-sizeably-intact second consignment of All Bran, which she had now been denied the time to murder. Well, I'm sure you're not going to grow fungus overnight, she thought decanting it back into the packet before marching straight for the door, whatever Garstone was rambling on about floating in her mind.

3

DEATH IN DÉJÀ VU

(i)

When Leyton had last read, police work *did* include apprehension of drivers cutting across public parks, as she often had to remind Garstone for un-mutual reasons. Having now trundled right across Green Oak Park's immense playing field to land amongst the usual gaggle of grubby unmarked units moored opposite the tennis court, she'd be understood for feeling something of a slight hypocrite.

"We're all guilty as hell of it this morning." Garstone mocked it, in a friendly way "Should see the grass verge outside my place, not that it *has* any grass now."
"Well, it sounds like there's something of a major attraction." Leyton tuned her ears into the waves of assorted voices over the other side "So when you're ready, MacDuff..."
"Ma'am," another familiar one called them from ahead "Come quick, tha' wants to check this out."

Wincing briefly at the newly installed aerial ropeway, which had displaced most of the vehicles onto the path she overtook her DC down the slope to where the chaotically overcrowded playground awaited. The pitifully rusted blue/pink railings looked unattractive enough to keep anyone away, allowing for the hardy lot that were Midelson Rd CID to work without disturbance. Not that those inside would notice, the barraging flashes from the scene photographers blinded people's eyes to all apart from what or who seemed the focus.

48

"We understand you finding this one a little familiar." Armitage felt it important as usual to warn her.

"All crimes are in *some* way, Leroy though most are five times that much unusual."

As the two officers at the gate lifted the tape up, Leyton knew she couldn't wait to see which category this one fell into, limbo-ing her way under the tape. Every head turned duly to herald her arrival with the usual royalty-oriented reverence, one exception of course being DCS Hargreaves but he seemed quite grateful.

"Made it on time for once, eh?" he muttered, flicking briefly around at her. "Looks like I can trust Garstone after all. Ergo, for your 'dedicated' application to your duties, it's... all yours."
He stepped aside and ushered the duo towards the swing.
"Okay you lot, shift, *she's* here."

Leyton was not used to the supercilious Hargreaves displaying actual manners on her behalf, but while semi-genuine the superintendent's lax attitude was, like often, down to a case of appearing more interested in his cigarettes than his coppers. Although long since illegal to light up on a crime scene, no one ever dared challenge Derek Hargreaves, even over this. Between puffs, he swapped a salacious glare with anyone he noticed staring, often blowing the ash back out in their direction like a badly temperamental dragon. Stories had reached Leyton: one member of St John's staff, not present today having been advised to 'eff off and work in an elderly care gaff instead' if he had an issue with the smoke.

As Hargreaves trudged away up the side of the playground turning his head, condescendingly as always at every cop stood about, she just shrugged and forged on with it.

The three forensic analysts gathered round the swing broke their circle to reveal to Leyton what had brought all and sundry to this peaceful community out on the sticks for the second time in as many mornings.

"Mmm… yes, this does ring a bit of a bell." hummed Leyton, right on cue.

Lying in the floor space between the two end swings, an adult figure lay twisted, his head fully turned on its side. One of the other officers appeared to be sheathing round the neck with a heavy set of pliers, aiming with difficulty at a shortish wire-like item virtually embedded into the chin.

"I assume it's not a chain this time then." she leant over to see.
"Suppose you could call it one," Armitage half-corrected. "Can say the blokes' bog's gonna take a job flushing from now."
"Hmm, small noose this time," she received the metre-long mesh portion. "How he managed to achieve it with such a meagre piece, I just don't…"

Muting her final word, she cradled the new-style 'chain' in her hand then noted the stature of the stiff's contortion once again, no mean feat considering how lopsided it lay, the head twisted firmly away like it were a toy action figure.

"And he looks too short in stature to have reached that from its original housing…"
"She some kind of expert on loos now, or summat?" Armitage whispered into Garstone's ear.
"Right, boys, less chit chat." Leyton commanded them like she were a movie director "Lets roll this poor fellow over."

All three lifted the body very carefully, as if restraining a boulder from the edge of a cliff. Suddenly it tumbled right on to its back, making Armitage jump away a bit as a white but noticeably bruised face lay staring up at him.

Significantly un-green looking for a person hung by his neck since the crack of dawn, Leyton judged the rest of his features, the relatively sporadic facial scars looking to have been imprinted during the earlier stages.

"This lucky guy goes by the name of Graham McMahon." Garstone leapt in "Aged 42, currently emp…"
"Just the name and age will do, Greg. Description also welcome, but I can handle so much at a time."

She looked closer at the deceased's face, moving back his collar-length bob. The left cheek and forehead above the right eye were heavily gashed, in such a way that it looked far from self-inflicted.

"Well unless he'd first walked in front of a car and didn't quite succeed, so thus proceeded to try ending it all this way…."
"What, ma'am?"

Armitage waited for her to finish but she'd suddenly felt an earlier issue still kicking angrily at the helm of her conscience.

"This is unbelievable." Leyton exclaimed in her famous high-pitched yelp. "Look at his face - not so much the scars, as the features. What do they remind you of?"
"Er like..."
Garstone looked at her then Armitage, little the wiser himself.
"Well, anything different from what we'd expect to get on a guy beaten about a bit, then dangled by a khazi pull?"
"I'll add this to the equation while you're deliberating."

Leyton definitely found the dead more informative than the living, this morning as she carefully pulled down the zip on Mr

McMahon's shell jacket. A darkish crimson top came into sight. The trio of vertical rips down the chest was the sickening first sight though it didn't leave any less red to be seen, - the ravaged flesh inside filled out the missing areas of shirt. Leyton saw this just before touching and withdrew her hands, hoping nobody had seen.

This guy has been dragged belly down by his feet along clearly rough ground; that could have been the killing process itself. Does this mean our suspect did his tricks by horse?

"We may have a medieval-style murderer here." she beckoned both of her perturbed DCs to view the mutilations "What does all this suggest to you?"
"Could actually be a Masonic job?" Armitage added in his guess.
"Masons don't normally come over as being the murderous type, Leroy," Leyton never welcomed empty assumptions. "Is this for once something you can back up?"
"Aye, quite easily."

He roped the other swing across. Etched into the seat was a deep-cut inscription. Though showing up poorly against the dark plastic, a circle was clear, fairly well applied though not enough to think a compass had been involved. Leyton placed her index finger at the middle, simulating a diagonal carve down to right. As if something had captured her concentration she repeated, albeit left, making out a further scratching of the like. *Another hieroglyph?* she wondered.

"It's a match with yesterday's." she announced swiftly to her chums "My believing that there is a lodge situated somewhere in Dore, I'd be the first to buy into your idea.... though this exact design has many possible associations."
"If it was a cult's thing," Garstone interrupted, "wouldn't it be in exactly the same place each time?" (*Yesterday it was etched into*

52

the floor about four feet away; this time we've got it on the swing itself)

"It's probable that he wanted it to be the last thing, his victim would see before he died. You'll forgive me if that's clichéd." (*That or per-HAPS because a wire end doesn't engrave concrete as effectively as a 500kg chain.*) She stood back up. "Right, would both of you kindly begin scribbling up on the similarities if you haven't already?"

Both men stopped, their faces adopting a puzzled look.

"Does my English sound a little off-kilter to you this morning then?" she offered to repeat the command.

"What those guys wanting here?" Garstone appeared to be distracted by a quartet of ambulance personnel closing in behind them. "We've only been here ourselves five minutes."

"Excuse me, ma'am,"

The senior paramedic cut in from behind, elbowing his way in, accompanied by three colleagues and began laying the body out in a roughly spread-eagled position.

"We need to get back now, I'm afraid,"

"Not until I've got the swing down," said Leyton.

She looked up hopelessly at the   middle swing, which was wrapped to the top of the bar, then at the sky up above it. That sunny spot Garstone had enjoyed was now lost behind a murky mid grey veil, slid across gloomily like a walk-in wardrobe door drawn back to shut out a handsome reflection.

"What you doing wi' that stuff?" Armitage enquired as the medics began unzipping the man's jacket and then lifting the shirt back.

"Seeing if we can get a bit more out of him," Hargreaves informed, having following the medics in.

"But, sir, he's dead. I thought you'd already settled on it."

"For the benefit of Messrs Garstone and Leyton" Hargreaves began with his cruelly patronizing voice "despite your uncharacteristically punctual arrival, we did actually happen to have a 'live one' when he was first stumbled upon by some unfortunate old dearie this morning?"

"And what did this... ahem, *elderly pensioner* you are referring to, manage to get out of him?" Leyton eagerly enquired.

"You're the one best asking her, Leyton, given your gift for conversing with coffin dodgers. Could barely make more sense of her, than *she* could of *McMahon*."

"If you tell me where I can find *her*, it would help."

"Armitage took her address when we first came up. Not that I'm thinking of letting you have it - she's been through enough today without you darkening her door."

Leyton dimmed her eyes momentarily at this distasteful slur, driven to the edge by Hargreaves's unhelpful, disparaging tone. He'd just nominated her as more the ideal one to initiate the questioning, then just as instantly, became candidly reluctant to tell her where Robbie's family could be contacted. How one could see to get the job done with his brutish decline of support, escaped her.

"How else am I supposed to find your 'star witness' then?" she heckled at him "Do I click my fingers and make her appear, or what?"

"Unless she's dashed back home in time to stop her scrambled egg boiling over, she should be sat by where you 'parked' your sad apology for a police vehicle."

"Okay."

Finding herself an opportunity to get away from the man for a few minutes, also handed to her on a plate by the very individual himself she made her way up the slope, and not alone.

"You mind if I join?" Garstone invited himself along

"Why would you do that Greg - to apply your 'special touch' again *or* also to flee the horrors of Hargreaves's world for a brief period?"

"Could say a bit o' both,"

Leyton batted her head in acknowledgement as Garstone followed behind. He could not help as he trekked past but notice the grass that was so deep in its colour that it looked like a giant green highlighter refill, exploded in the heavens with impeccable enough aim to completely miss the path.

"Hello..."

That woman's voice stole him straight back from his fascinations yet again. It was not he that Leyton was soliciting the attention of this time, though.

(ii)

"I believe you've got a story to tell us."

Leyton addressed the little figure, sat on a bench, back up near the car. The colossal fur coat, from which a lilac-hatted head emerged, had grown into a one-man tent as she'd shrunk with age. The small pink face amongst it looked out as if watching from a hole, her silver hair only possible to see when she faced to her side.

"Ooh, I don't think it's really that much of a story, dear." she replied displaying little shock in her tone, "I just found a man underneath the swing. Seen it before."

"What, a dead one?"

Leyton seemed to have already identified the woman, 86-year-old Mrs Skelton of Shuttlethorpe Close, renowned as a regular-park goer for the past three decades since retirement. Always with a tale to tell, she'd seen more in Totley in one week than people saw in a whole country, probably enough even to run a daily bulletin.

"Dead? Oh dearie. I never knew he'd finally passed."
"On the basis of that reaction, what I've heard about you finding Mr McMahon alive sounds to add up."
"He was talking. Very weak though, - was as if he was being strangled."
"Well, the fact that we found his neck wrapped tightly by a makeshift toilet chain might have had something to do with that. You certainly miss very little, don't you?"
"Oh, I don't remember that."
"Can we talk about what you *do* remember, for a minute - I rightly gather you had siphoned a few words out of Mr McMahon before he expired altogether."
"Only a couple, not much. I said before, he had trouble talking, the poor lad."
"What were they, can you remember at all?"
"Oh, I think...oh hang on."

The elderly lady punctuated practically all lines beginning with *oh* or *well* by leaning forward with both hands over the top of her marble walking stick handle. It was her indication of *hold on, love, I need to think about this one* but she was always genuine to the letter with everything she said, looking Leyton straight in the eye, through the octagonal glasses that rested off the tip of her nose.

"What was it he said now, your Mr *Hargrave*, he took it down."
"*Hargreaves*?!!" Leyton far from happy to hear that name turned

to Garstone, "This doesn't mean we've got to beg *that* off him, now?"

"We could pop back round and try." Garstone became optimistic "We've already got ourselves in his good books once today."

"That's it," the pensioner's face brightened up "that's what the lad said. 'Round'."

"*Round?*"

"Yes... *round and*...erm....something that sounded like '*round*' again. He repeated it about three times, I remember."

"Let's just assume for the time being it was 'round and round'." Leyton decided confidently "I can't imagine for now what else it would have been, Mrs..."

"Skelton. Elaine Skelton."

"Thankyou Mrs Skelton, nice to meet someone so willing to help, especially when it involves divulging information with.... *him.*"

Leyton found the temptation to bad-mouth that Stone-age relic of a Superintendent, in the presence of the public almost impossible to defy by now. Regardless of her current relationships with certain higher officers, she contained it by the skin of her teeth, though only to adhere to profession.

Either a detective in disguise or just a local busybody trying to prove her attention-grabbing came with justification, Mrs Skelton's attitude was proving something of an endearing boost to Leyton's lightning-swift enquiries even if a few of the 'wise old woman's lines proved a little unspecific to start.

"Hey!" Garstone interrupted "Shall I go see what else they've found, before he puts the 'magic white tent' up?"

"Okay, Greg. They might have caught a suspect by now."

"Oh there'll be plenty to pick from round here, love," Mrs Skelton seemed ready to assist such a pleasant pair of detectives to the limit of capability, "Kids, mostly. No respect, none of them."

"Kids?! Which sort exactly -I do expect there to be a few in this vicinity at half term." "Kids you know...what's the word you use these days...er, 'yobbos', that's it- you know, them lads with the hooded jumper things on."

Mrs Skelton continued as she did the action of putting a hood over her head to translate to Leyton, what she herself was quite easily beginning to picture.

An abrupt amalgam of boys' voices and bicycle pedals alerted her to three youths who bombed it down from the bowling green, narrowly missing where Mrs Skelton sat.

"Hey!" Leyton called, outraged at blatant hooliganism like this.
"Shit! Pigs!" shouted one of the boys, seeing the cars moored in the background.
"Greg..." Leyton spittled into the radio "Can you please get straight up here and keep Mrs Skelton company?"
She nodded quickly at the pensioner before tearing across the grass after the three BMXs.

Making use of the tyre-trodden spur engineered by incoming authority vehicles, she hoped the near-hardened mud would prove durable under her stilettos.

Catching up with the trio of yobs as they cruised arrogantly along the top path, she could reach out and grab the rear rider, his distinctive pudding-bowl cut and the cream *Adidas* sweater standing out suspiciously. Unfortunately her shoes seemed unable to adapt to the change in floors. As she moved to get her net down, before the gate out to Mickley Lane the youth defiantly swerved, luring her straight across a patch of frozen dew.

The resulting twist of direction sent her diving painfully to the floor. Leyton sensed an almighty sledgehammer colliding with her leg. After cursing sweet nothings she hoped Mrs Skelton didn't pick up on, she brought herself back up to her feet, only then feeling her latest bruises at their worst and hobbled her way back up the path, all the weight piled on her good leg instead.

"Leroy, Greg..." she spluttered down the Ericsson, starved for breath, "Unit to top street, fast! Three youths on bikes, one familiar!"
(Only *ONE young man would try something that stupid round here today.*)
"Whereabouts up top, ma'am?" went Armitage "Baslow Road's hardly just a couple of yards."
"Use your imagination, just make it snappy. They're hardly likely to stay and mosey round, the whole day. Before you move, let our medical mates know they may have an extra patient here."

Doubting Armitage knew what she was harping on about, Leyton rapidly heaved herself to the top of the path, her call having already having seen her reach the bowling house. She hoped that the half-term week kept those toilets at the back open for today at least.

Feeling trapped, not just by his obligation to assist Leyton but also where he was, by Hargreaves - a man known to (violently) manhandle wayward cops back to the workplace - Armitage tiptoed past and out, crouched amongst Thompson, Hall and Pelhandri as they also responded to the DI's plight.

"Flamin' idle flatfoots." the superintendent shook his head, taking thankfully little notice "wouldn't understand real police work if it were dropped on their dinner."

He turned back round again, catching Garstone also making to leap the railings.

"Somewhere you're going, sonny?"

"DI says a kid's nearly just took Mrs Skelton's head off, on his pedal bike… guess who?"

"Bennington?! Bring me the little bastard's head on a plate, Greg you hear me? Leave your girlfriend tending to the grannies."

Tired of listening to his limitless bigotry, he left to deal with it though Leyton at the moment was concerned with her physical pains more than her emotional ones. The assorted septuagenarians warming up for their weekly bowling meet nearby, looked equally enveloped in their activities to see her. The outside serving hatch was a refreshing sight, until she found the shutter still unopened. Helpless to whisper anyone over for a minute of their assistance, Hall's siren sadly only made it harder as the unit began on their offensive behind the houses.

As they flew up Green Oak Avenue to the top, warily straying over the wrong side of 30mph Armitage also disagreed with the noise. Seeing a cut-through to the main street, Hall stopped up fast at the kerbside.

"Co-Op store, round the corner!" he instructed Pelhandri and Thompson "Loads of bikes piled outside, erratically should be a giveaway."

As both PCs vacated to give chase, Hall set off over down Lemont Road hoping to cut the yobs off from all angles.

"Shut that bloody thing off," Armitage urged his driver "I want to gi' 'em a surprise."

Hall, the team's most procedural member reluctantly downed the sirens, especially disliking it when Armitage needed to do things differently.

Fooled less by the silence, Leyton set her ears for an immediate second blast from over the terraced rooftops, the stagnant chimney soot lingering above torturous enough... along with her leg.

While waiting an extremely long minute for it to start again, a couple of less distant metallic clunks suddenly turned her to facing the pavilion, or perhaps the far side of it. (*A bicycle chain,*) she guessed strongly (*can't be from inside the kitchen, surely*)

The noise again, fainter but it made up her mind. Her own, old machine's mechanism could vouch with the sound it used to give on jumping a sprocket.

Sidling along the front of the bowling house, Leyton cut her movement, backing her ear up against the splintery green shutter. She shuffled discreetly along, reaching the corner of the building and cautiously began the final movement of stepping round, ready to face her targets.

"Oh god, I hope Chris is in position," she thought to herself, having not heard any sirens yet. (*Here goes...*)

Leyton threw herself into the full view of the drive.

Not a figure or bike stood anywhere.

(*Has got to be the Co-op then,*) she finalised in her own conscience (*...hang on, it's that sound.*)

She whirled around to face the house. A very faint tinkle again, unmistakable as that of a bicycle, came to her from somewhere very nearby.

61

Leyton returned herself to the wall, the risk of fungi connecting with her pricey suit jacket, currently irrelevant. Again, she tried moving slowly along, listening all the way. Further recurrences of the sound soon answered her just as last time, right on the other side of this here wall. Working herself round the corner, something on the floor outside the men's toilet doorway, made her look down.

Bicycle tyre marks laced the tiled floor below her - indeed of the same brown as the mud that had just sent her tumbling. Tracing them back a distance, they trailed in from the gateway, right round past the recycling bins and straight beneath her feet into...*that's it. They're hiding in the bloody loo*, she reckoned.

Then 'that sound' again, and now with it, a voice - that of a young teenage male, which while only *just* audible gave the game away for Leyton. She had this tearaway's technique completely rumbled now. (*Make havens in the one place a female police officer might probably deem as off-limits.*) Well, *this* female police officer was constructed of sterner fibre. Feeling in her jacket for her favourite little card, she slithered along towards the toilet doorway, maintaining extreme silence.

Leyton took one final breath, by now having given up on Armitage showing up in time, and swung round in through the entrance, throwing her arm almost violently round the intruder's shoulder.

"Okay, you little bast..."

The grey-clad youngster parked halfway into the toilet cubicle, looked up at her.

Garstone always found his current DI to be something of a handful but this time it was nearly literal. Heaving her into the bowling clubroom over his shoulder, he asked Thompson to run the kettle and fetch a wet flannel back, before lowering Leyton onto a chair.

"Where's Leroy got to?" she nagged, pulling up her trouser leg to see the damage. "I thought I'd told him to get back right away."

A flush of the toilet next door answered.

"Right, *madam*..." Garstone wrenched the flannel under the cold tap "this had better not be too messy, or it's to the medical office for you."

He walked over and sat opposite. On lifting her leg round by the calf, to see it for himself the injury appeared fairly minimised. A violet swell of the inner ankle just above the heel plus a faint golf ball-sized graze beneath the knee seemed the limit. Garstone slowly gave her the flannel, ensuring she placed it right on the swollen spot before he stopped watching her.

"Hold it there two minutes, ma'am. Just gonna see to the kettle." He dived back across to the service hatch. "Will, throw me the first aid gear."

As Leyton waited, she let the preserved jade/white blend of the bowling room interior take her mind off it, ironically the same environment her father sat within for many a year while priming his woods for the Wrangleford greens. The semi-boarded walls echoed not only her voice and Thompson's rattling of teaspoons, but more importantly, memories of herself as a young pig-tailed 5-year old waddling in to meet her daddy after his game on Sunday afternoon.

"I were amazed I managed to flush that thing wi' out a chain on it any more." said Armitage, entering in time to wreck her moment of reflection.
"Well we all know where that's gone don't we?"

Leyton shuffled about underneath Garstone's coat hunting for the marked packet containing the wire removed from Mr McMahon's neck, but couldn't find it laying there.

"That's funny. You did say you'd taken that 'chain' from the scene, Leroy."
"Hopefully, they're adjusting it for your miserable gullet instead, Leyton."

Hargreaves, having followed in behind Armitage, stood there roaring his latest in natural insults though on this occasion with possible reason. He stepped right in and stood over her, though Leyton was more concerned with following the good Dr Garstone's advice than enduring his abuse.

"Oh dear you went quite a treat there didn't you," he surveyed the bruising "I hope that hurts like hell, that's all I can say - time something taught you a lesson."
"And of what disservice have I been to you this time, sir?"
"Absconding a murder scene to go chasing an innocent kid into the bog, and then dragging him from his bike - would that do? Obviously it won't but…"
"Sir, that 'lad' rode straight across a bowling green - illegally."
"Ok, there's no need to talk back."
"I wasn't. I said I just happened to be standing right there, questioning Mrs Skel."

"I said *DON'T TALK BACK*!" Hargreaves erupted viciously, his face reddening momentarily enough for Leyton to back down. "About time you learned the way it is in here, Little Miss Busybody!"

He rested his palms firmly on his legs, squatting forward to address Leyton eyeball-to-eyeball. As unhappy with her as he could already get in just two days, he wasn't prepared for further nonsense, or to mess around himself.

"You think you can just do what you like and when you like, don't you? Well I'm here to tell you how pitifully deluded you are, DI Lame Skull. The crack is this. My department, my rules - at this stage, you have broken ninety-nine percent of them."
"She was just using initiative sir." said Thompson "Police officers do tend to."
"Funnily enough, initiative and your opinion have got something in common, PC Thompson. I only want them when I ask for them. So piss off and try catching that kid Leyton's managed to scare away!"

Thompson, a notably emotional young man at times left the room, his face turned puffy-eyed from having been yelled at unexpectedly by a man who often praised his work. Hargreaves infamously reserved his sadistic soccer-coach manner towards younger members, as well as public-schooled thirtysomething policewomen yet on seeing this in its fully appalling practice, Leyton was not prepared to sit there and watch him take his frustrations with her out on someone else.

"Why don't *I* talk to those kids, sir? Aren't I the one who caused them their fright?"
"If it turns out that little turd you let go without my permission last night is an associate of theirs, we've managed to scare the whole village shitless of the police."

"Sir, that's wrong," Leyton protested. "Their appearance was circumstantial."

"Stop talking back, woman! I won't warn you again!"

Hargreaves prodded his left finger into her face, almost literally so, then stood and walked away, giving Thompson a derisory sneer as he stepped in by. Garstone had a better idea for his DI anyway than hang around with that bigoted pleb of a Superintendent breathing down on them.

"Reckon we ought to drop by Danny's place for a word?" he asked, casually hoping Leyton would accept. "There's always a chance those kids are linked with his lot."

Though she made sense of the suggestion, Leyton answered silently as Hargreaves re-appeared in the doorway.

"Do you think I go suddenly deaf outside, Garstone?"

He marched in, eyes blazing, hollering at both of them like a drill sergeant on a bad day. Hargreaves had clearly not had enough of bullying his favourite *least favourite* today. He cut his volume but continued.

"He's only suggesting we have a scour round the area sir, just hoping we may find them still around."

"They've gone HOME, Leyton, the same place you're going. Consider yourself removed from the scene with immediate effect. I pick up that you've so much as attempted to speak to Bennington without my saying so, and your precious badge will be the reason my loo's still blocked on Saturday morning."

Hargreaves glared at her again to ensure it sunk all the way in. As soon as his back was turned, heading out of the door, Garstone swung up a tall two-fingered salute, mouthing words he'd rather not say out loud in front of a lady.

"Come on; let's get out before he cooks up an excuse to chuck you the full way."

Leyton sprung to her feet and as the flannel fell off, the pain re-ignited twice as sharply, making Hargreaves' roasting of superficial concern.

"I should have warned you to get up slowly," sighed the DC.

4

OFF THE CASE

(i)

While both Leyton and Armitage's supposedly legitimate absences from the Midelson Rd briefing room, this lunchtime left only nine other officers in attendance that was above full, all the same for any conference led by DCS Hargreaves.

Keeping anyone and everyone away from wanting to occupy the front chairs, the superintendent's putrid tobacco odour was drowned away by something doubly offensive, as he munched his cheese sandwich between marking the whiteboard. Although officers present felt even more forced to maintain their distance, the smell could have more likely so followed him along the corridor that plastic bread bag on his desk having become Britain's deadliest pollution hazard it is five years of daily usage.

(*£400k blown on refurbishing the bastard, and they let that hypochondriac loose on it*) Garstone faced part towards the whiteboard, deliberately as not to look straight at him, his lips almost moving aloud with thought.

Pcs Raylesthorpe, Hall, Pelhandri and an assortment of detective personnel plus crime scene officer Sergeant Barnes whispered small nothing amongst themselves, swapping pans and notepads, very much in an arrived-here-at-the-very-last-minute-manner. The smell was probably not what the other cops were discussing amongst more important things - stumped as to why their most trusted leader was missing.

Rubbing Garstone's face in a situation he felt very ashamed to explain, not one look of contempt actually came his way from the crowd, the only two to merely harbour any respect towards Hargreaves being DS Burkinshaw and DCC Etchley from Don Valley HQ. Three of Midelson's top floor boys, Sgt Agworubu, DCs Long and McGavin did not relish arriving downstairs only to find themselves sat facing DCS Hargreaves in place of the remarkable woman they were nowadays used to leading the way.

Respected for working humbly alongside whoever he was forced to put up with, Garstone was one man alone disgusted in secret at Hargreaves's handpicking favouritisms when it came to him filling the seats. So many were selected doubtlessly due to personal friendliness - he still had them amongst his many enemies - or also punishment and perhaps favours he believed certain officers still owed. Derek Hargreaves was a man who never forgot let alone forgave those who trod on his toes, each and every copper in this room kept as a prisoner to his principle.

Garstone, the only man in the room assigned to this case already could not afford to let his own image be clouded, stood alongside the corrupt superintendent. As a token of his comparative professionalism, he expanded the details, so far across to the right-hand board for the benefit of Barnes's deteriorating eyesight, the ageing sergeant probably just one more optician's visit away from forced retirement.

Finding another regular stench to contend with, he held the marker at arm's length, its spirit ink offering quite a scent for a non-permanent.

"Are you quite ready yet, Rolf Harris?" rudely interrupted the DCS "No disrespect to you son, but some people haven't had their dinner yet."
"Okay, okay…"

Garstone didn't intend a fall-out in front of his peers, getting on with the show straight away, secretly though hoping it would conclude prematurely.

"So, right guys, this is what we've got on our plates today…"

He stood aside, directing them through the information inked below the victims, though could not help but end up reciting it in its entirety to appease Barnes again.

"Mr Ecclesby and Mr McMahon - two local males, both aged in their early-mid forties, both murdered in the small hours yesterday and today respectively… *both* methods as same, bar the sight detail." He encouraged them to overlook the minor variation in nooses for now. "Although we have co-operative witnesses on both scenes, who claim - at least in one case - to have found the victim still a fraction with us, no visible items of physical evidence have yet been pulled up by either sweep."

Stopping him, he saw the officers scratching their heads, pads placed down as they looked past Garstone to the board.

"Strategy and preparation, I think are the words Mr Garstone's stuck for." Hargreaves did him a sudden favour for once though it did divert the younger cop from further elaborating on his current topic. "He obviously took nothing along, except the tasty set of latex mits he'd wear for the deed - his weapon was sat waiting above him."

Hargreaves tapped his pointer at the swing, Garstone noticing that some of his own hand-drafted detail had vanished from the board.

"Dusting the entire frame over didn't return anything, I assume,"

Barnes added to his support, "I neglected to pester the forensics properly before leaving."

"DNA has drawn a total blank in either case as yet, Sarge," Garstone confessed.

"It's *sir* to you." Hargreaves brashly mouthed beside him.

"Whatever." he moved along, not giving a damn for once, "Neither of the two scenes have turned up a single thumb print so far, therefore landing us at the back of an awkwardly high hurdle."

"That means the tool used to cut the chain is going to be untraceable as well," Barnes rubbed it in.

"He did leave one tiny memoir in his wake."

Garstone was reminded again thanks to the 'tool' reference. He drew the strange 'A' -sign on the board, treeing it to both scenes.

"Found at each scene, etched into hard floor immediately below the victim's body... something wrong, Chris?"

PC Hall was looking unsurely at the board. Hargreaves had placed a murkily indecipherable A4 print over the logo.

"I think this should be easier for them to read, don't you?" he sneered at Garstone.

"Sir, they can't see anything," he pointed out the almost unintelligible shape on the paper.

"This is a murder scene briefing, not a bloody archery class, Garstone."

He spat at the board to remove a tiny bit of the drawing still remaining, and then turned to continue, only for Hall to fire his next arrow faster.

"Irrespective of this, Greg - though I do not ignore its irrelevance - does geographical proximity of the two deaths verifiably indicate motive?"

"In a way." Garstone hated to tear an intelligent question apart, given as they send like gold at the moment. "We are strongly pressed to believe at this stage that this happened on pretence of repetitive mistaken identity."

"In English," Hargreaves started, translating it as something completely separate "the suspect does not seem scared to strike in almost the same place twice."

"*Work of a local* is the best way round it, lads." said Garstone, drawing a near -professional looking area outline of Totley on the board. He put a line in, joining the two murders as a trail. "Someone who's clued up on what's *where*, and doesn't need a map with him. Guilt may have even moved our guy a little more adrift this time."

The seated cops passed a strange look to the board once more as Garstone waited for questions.

Hargreaves stood back, having instantly wiped the DC's map away, replacing it with two appallingly drawn squares separated by a scale's line, minus the line of connection. Garstone cursed at his DC's despicable brashness, hurriedly re-adapting scene details into the re-drawn version as best as he could squash them.

"Now, the two victims themselves," he started boldly into a bigger topic. "Both single males, no immediate next of kin, though believed local residents. Mr Ecclesby and Mr McMahon could be soliciting homosexuals who just got 'unlucky. I know this is a blunter opinion than you or particularly DI Leyton expect from me normally, but their being in a public park alone at time of death doesn't quickly make either out as completely innocent."

"More to the point, being in a playground may say to you it wasn't actually blokes they were after."

"Neither Ecclesby or McMahon have a criminal history currently under file."

"Could always be just some toffee-nosed do-gooder ducked behind the wall."

"Now, this is in contrast to the DCS own previous theory as well as mine..." he faced the audience "Still, shit happens all the ...same..."

Garstone stopped to think about this amidst confusion, hesitant as he looked at the whiteboard. His boss's rapid-fire reiterations of every item he'd discussed, this last twenty minutes was finally slowing him hard in his tracks.

"Something else stopping you, son?" The superintendent never missed a thing going off around him.

Garstone certainly caught the latest sinister smell, that of sudden male flatulence. The guilty look came right of both their faces as Hargreaves swept the board of all but the photos.

"Euurrgh!" Garstone made sure he heard him.

"What do you mean *ugh-oh-arggh!!!*" Hargreaves dropped his cloth "is that you?"

"Er, yeah." He cautiously answered though knew it was actually the superintendent, deep down. "Sorry about that, sir."

"Well don't stand there like a crying schoolkid," he blasted into Garstone's ear. "There's a loo right through the door. Also, best call it a day if I were you - don't want additional tear gas in the station."

The DCS angrily pointed him straight out.

"YES-S-S!!" Garstone said immediately on closing the door.

He tiptoed across into the disabled lavatory doorway, waiting for

WPC Harsingh to pass along without catching him, and then closed the door. Rattling the toilet seat, he counted to a very slow thirty then flushed before sneaking out and heading to the station canteen.

(ii)

Leyton seized as the final blob of antiseptic was applied over the purpling gash. Although the dressing was intended as a first aid implement, the corrosive sensation turned it to just the opposite. It also brought a tear to the eye of WPC Raymond who was doing the duty here. The ageing station officer, who didn't exactly secret her fondness for Midelson Road's star cop could hardly bear to see any injury to her protégé, though made her thoughts open that Garstone's offer of help at the bowling green had been a bad choice.

"I'm so glad they told you to come to me, instead duck,"

She repetitively commented, rubbing the stuff in before reaching for the three quarter metre stretch of bandage she'd cut ready And didn't Leyton know it - if it had been Hargreaves she'd shown her bruises to, he'd have just told her to piss off back home and hold it under the tap for about half an hour - preferably the boiling hot one.

"Don't worry," Leyton finally had it in her to shut her up, "the biggest sting's come from Hargreaves today, as usual."

She filled her in on the morning's events that had landed her prematurely back at HQ. That boy she'd encountered in the Green Oak Park loo turned out not to be Danny Bennington in the end, despite the likeness. Apologies from herself and

74

Garstone followed to the youth but her boss was never about to let it pass as a superficial foul up. No less the common Neanderthal of a cop, Hargreaves had hurled his book straight at her in that bowling hut, as she now spelt the dispiriting story out again for Raymond.

Although the DCS didn't seem prepared to show it straight, Leyton's mollycoddling of Robbie Draycott had only worsened his distrust in her another complete stride down the ladder, the rungs of which were, by now getting precariously wobbly. Thank hell, he hadn't heard about her sneaky trip back to Dore last night though that was something she still wouldn't want Garstone to know of just yet either.

"We all make mistakes, lovey." the WPC naively evaluated her plight.
"Yes though he wishes I'd make a bigger one, probably. Either way, I'm off the case for the rest of the day, due to my sins."
"*WE* are off, you mean, Miss L?"

Both women's attention was drawn to a familiar young man standing in the doorway, one hand resting in his jacket pocket, the other waving guiltily. The ever-caring DC Garstone stuck to Leyton like glue and only not knowing where she'd disappeared to from her office on arrival back from Totley delayed his entry.

"Not that I'm exactly gonna question Hargreaves' orders to his face," he began cynically, "but if you think I'm gonna see you sent out on your todd while I gruel with that bastard, alone..."
"*He's got another thing coming*, or several, we hope. You're a sweet man, Greg Garstone. It's just a pity Leroy didn't also take the opportunity,"
"Speaking of *taking*" WPC Raymond interrupted, "Would you fancy taking a quick walk, ma'am so I can assess my handiwork?"

"I suppose I must at some stage," Leyton agreed, "assuming everyone's now had a good look - eh Greg?"

Garstone pretended not to know who her moment of humour was aimed at as she stood up and lowered her trouser back swiftly, almost snagging the plaster. Taking a few steps forwards and rotating round, Leyton tried to get used to the feel of her currently restricted ability of movement.

"Are you still okay to drive, love?" the older WPC continued to quiz her.
"I hope so!" Garstone insisted on it being the case "…seeing as we've got the remaining nine tenths of the investigation ahead."

A hint came to light that his leader remained at liberty, to ply her trade elsewhere in the case. Yet stuck without the mounds of further information she could have collected had that caveman of a DCS not thrown her off the scene by her ear, a different starting point had to be created.

"Leroy pulled another couple of things from Mr McMahon while the Super' had his back turned. Nothing great to look at, apart from a few business cards."
"Well, where are they? I can hardly look at them from here."
"If it saves you the job for now, one entry suggests he was a recent visitor at Gipton's Motors, er…here we go, *No 1… Talltree Farm, Owler Bar.*"
"There's a print error if ever I saw one. The place in mention is actually off Penny Lane, Old Hay."
"That's pretty impressive coming from someone who's only lived here six months. Perhaps he got murdered for giving the wrong direction."

Leyton could not help but find this one at least a little funny, before twirling on her bad ankle in reaction caught her cropper.

"Whoops," she straightened herself just in time "I nearly gave *myself* the wrong ones there."

"I'd best be careful today then…."

Garstone knew he wasn't going to get out of it, and dived back into the office. Checking there was no Hargreaves about, he helped himself to the envelope of small personal effects recovered from *McMahon M - Totley 28-10-10* and having dug out the Gipton's call card, made hastily for the photocopier. An unwelcome delay came courtesy of the machine's two-minute warm-up process, causing him to look round behind him, literally the entire time. The job finally done, he got it put back in, trying to remember the package's exact position before dashing back to Leyton.

With the 'walking test' completed, she was stood outside the first aid room as he returned, but instead of accepting the photocopy gratefully gasped as she saw Hargreaves strolling behind him, returning from the canteen. The Superintendent ignored her gesture but paused before stepping into the CID room.

"Feeling any better, Garstone? Thought you'd have had the sense to go home."

"Aye, I'm just taking her," Garstone mockingly eased him. "She's not quite in the   best of ways for driving."

Hargreaves didn't say anything else, just shutting himself and his grunts inside the office.

"Right…." the DC pointed towards the double doors at the end, "Let's get rolling, lady."

"Did I tell you that I'd been here before, about three months ago?" Leyton said as she enjoyed another passenger-seat ride.

Although the leg still stung, she secretly loved every minute of it, as she directed Garstone. Turning right onto Penny Lane, he kept his thoughts on a certain Beatles number to himself, only for Leyton to spoil his effort by humming it. Visiting the countryside on the job was a treat for her, even with a wintry landscape outside the window as Garstone escorted her into the towering green depths of Totley Moors. Getting to see it at all had been a rare experience in Cambridgeshire, despite having it almost on her doorstep. Leyton's work kept her almost reserved for urban cases, and with her dad barely able to walk since retiring, strolls with the family dog became less appealing.

Rural a place as it might have kept, Wrangleford was barely much more a crime-free haven than Sheffield, come night (and the day after). The 'posh', university-educated stereotypes that Hargreaves amongst millions others came to associate the place with barely existed today; by 2003, in the midst of Blair's Britain 'hoodies', 'chavs' and hooligans were all over the streets like ants.

Her image of the place she'd left half-a-year ago now, as how she once knew it as a child was closely pictured in this leafy end of Sheffield nearing the Derbyshire boundary. The isolated community of Totley Old Village embodied a few cottages, cricket ground and single pub plus umpteen farms, mostly abandoned, though it remained a well kept little community with picturesque gardens and healthy trees shooting up in abundance, the welcome vegetation concealing the tunnel shafts that tarnished the horizon.

"*Just about there* she says…" Garstone soon put a stop to her forbidden merriment. "We've gone past half a dozen farms in Old Hay already. Now you're telling me I've got on the wrong bloody road, like?"

"I'd have said that by now - I'm not that horrid."

[It's just a case that I can't quite recall every single gate peeping out from between a hedge and a clump of infinitely untrimmed birch trees that a pair of muddy tyre tracks draws me toward.]

"Well you said *up here*. Guessin' you never chased a thief in a tractor before, then?"

"Can't say I have. If you're accusing me of some sudden inability to differentiate between tractor and car tyres, Greg I found your earlier joke about Mr McMahon's death even funnier."

"There's a way to tell the two apart don't forget. Tractors would only go in and out once a day, cars probably a bit more often."

He a halted to an opening, near the top of the lane. A reasonable variety of tread patterns, some recent while others appeared faded with age, decorated the concrete in colours ranging from black to light brown and even something resembling green.   Lumps of goose excrement amongst them made Garstone regret studying the ground just yet.

"I should trick my resident car-expert into taking the wheel more often," she noted the near-camouflaged oak board reading '*TALL TREES FARM 1-7*'.

Before she had time to interpret the white/blue sign underneath it, beyond an initial 'G', Garstone heaved the Vectra sharply onto the gravel-layered road leading them further into the forest.

Leyton's colleague immediately suspected a prank was intended in tricking him into driving back in the same direction they had just come, via a different route, until a small village of houses and large wooden stable conversions appeared from amongst the trees.

"Don't they remind you of somewhere?"
Garstone pointed in front as a couple of geese waddled slowly past in front.
"Yes, but there's just two of them this time."
Ignoring her, he fired a ripple of parps lasting for about five seconds.
"Greg, don't."
"It's alright. Geese and I have a good understanding...Oh, looks like I've saved us the trouble of knocking."

A man in a canary jumpsuit stood outside the top garage at left. The middle-aged figure looked uninvitingly on this new rival in the yard, a near smile on his face fading as he assessed the description of the car, and its occupants.

"Suppose he might have thought he had a queue of customers arriving here instead of a couple of police officers? Oh Greg, you rotter, raising his hopes like that."
"Well with us blocking the way, he's not going to get anywhere."
"Unless he's got an escape hatch."

She pointed to where the man had just been standing but had now vanished as if he were a mirage.

"Let's just park up and see if he can hel...look out."

A huge female sheepdog came lumbering out of No6, one of the adjoining farmhouses and went almost straight into the trajectory of the Volkswagen. The suddenly over-alert Garstone slammed the brake on, but the screeching came instead from her rather angry owner. As the creature answered to its master's call, the farmer's wife gave Garstone and his superior a momentary look of notable hostility before closing her door.

"Well if that's the welcome we get from the neighbour..." Leyton insinuated as he pulled up to the side.

She hinted that the shortage of warm receptions towards the police, in these parts might relate to her other trip out this way back in July, also then a passenger in Garstone's Vectra. Did one of Tall Trees Farm's other residents perhaps recognise her from that time?

"You reckon I ought to introduce myself to the guy first?"
"If he's still around - it might actually be wiser, considering he shares your passion for cars."

They made their way across the manure-caked forecourt towards the doorway of No1, standing proud below its shiny blue banner. Easing the corrugated door open enough to slip in unheard, Garstone reluctantly ushered in ahead by Leyton side-stepped into the murky but well-kept looking garage that awaited them.

"Hey mate, you in?"

Straining it barely above a whisper he listened out extremely carefully which for him was a rarity. The impression that this business and its premises were now abandoned could not be much longer avoided. Notable too was how neatly stacked the tools and machines were on the side as if they had been packed away ready for selling or transportation. Placing this firmly into perspective, it occurred that this man they'd just spotted could have been expecting bailiffs.

Garstone weighed up both ways how instinct worked here, one of the first things taught even a naive creature like himself from day one being *'guilt makes a person run!'* A sudden return of footsteps interrupted his fantasies once more, this time more those of DI Leyton than a shifty motor mechanic. Just so he knew, she poked her head round the end of the transit.

"Found something interesting, Greg?"
"Looks like he's thinking of going away somewhere, the way he's got this place. An independent car mechanic stuck out the back-hole of nowhere, you'd think. Right tidy lookin', like."
"If you want me to look at her, son, there's no use leaving it parked out there." a third voice impeded their discussion. "I've only got lights indoors at this place."
"Oh, so you *are* still in."

Leyton displayed what gratitude she could muster for the indication that they were not alone in the room.

"And whereabouts are you exactly?"
"Straight ahead, unless you need glasses." came the response.

Leyton peeped her head round the Transit once more and could just make out some sort of movement. Looking with her viewpoint adjusted slightly further adrift, the corner tip of a yellow-clad elbow could just be seen bobbing around slightly.

"Oh, hello."

She raised her voice to full speaking level for the first time since entering. The shape in front of her, lent over a table was clearly the same man from outside.

"You'll excuse me for not turning," the stranger raised his own tone a little to level with hers. "I'm just finding it difficult to look at people face-to-face, with having lost my friend today."
"Oh dear. And who might that b…what?"

She caught a soft nudge from Garstone on her shoulder. Looking to her right, the afternoon's *Star* newspaper sat folded on a table, its title and headline looking straight up at her. The first three words she saw took the form of '*SECOND SWING MURDER*'.

"New travels fast," she picked up the tabloid for a closer look.
"It was actually a DCS Hargreaves who told me. I rang Mr McMahon up this morning to let him know his vehicle motor be ready for about four-ish. I got this chap on the line instead, told me that he'd 'have a little trouble answering the phone as from now on.'"
"Well, that's Superintendent Hargreaves' line in condolences."
"Oh thanks for correcting me - you've as good as admitted to being the police yourselves."
"Afraid so."

Leyton didn't want to have to wave the badge at him, any more than he did. Ray Gipton felt the police were round to push their enquiries on them in the commonly intense manner, treating witnesses and offenders almost equally as badly. Plucking up the courage finally to turn round to his visitors, the eye contact lasted not even momentarily. He sat down on a half-pulled out stool and buried his head briefly before talking.

"I could do with knowing what he was doing in a kiddies' playground anyway, without any children in his company?"
"Well that's saved us the job of asking our first question,"
Leyton felt a twinge of recklessness in her conscience as she asked this.
"What I meant was, he's got no contact with his kids nowadays, not since him and his wife split up."
"He hasn't had any sort of trouble with the law has he, that would associate with his body turning up in such a place?"
"No, can't think of any; I mean, like me he preferred men to

minors."

She silenced herself again as a more definite picture of this gentleman began to take shape. His unusually softly and well-spoken manner for a person of his occupation had already given Leyton cause to ponder his sexuality but she had further questions ready. She let the next go for a second having seen he was looking at her with a glossy stare.

"Do you have a problem with standing, Miss Leyton?"

Ray was eyeing the way she leant rather precariously against the ill-fitted shelving unit, her worse leg resting on the floor by her toe.

"You could say so, well on one ankle today at least."
"There's a chair behind you there." He pointed under the end of the desk, also asking Garstone, to a polite shake of the head.
"Greg's always a man for standing." said Leyton. "You'll rarely catch him with his bum on a seat, even in an interview room."

Garstone deciding on maintaining that stance, she tried making herself comfortable on the small plastic chair, quite likely some local playgroup throw-out. The savagely cracked blue seat forced her to squat right on the edge instead.

"Mr Gipton, I 'm wondering, like…if you don't mind me asking," Garstone got there first, nearly tripping his words as always. "What made you set up shop out here in the middle of nowhere?"
"Er…"

Ray tried to track through his mind, though it didn't look fully convincing to either of the cops. Constant frustrated gripping of his pencil of his pencil in his left hand as he sat with his face hidden spelt threads of potential guilt as his hesitant responses and shortage of eye contact persisted. Leyton remained distrustful; also building up a count of the times he'd bent down to pick that imaginary screw off the floor. Signs like these were second nature to her capabilities in guilt detection but her doubts were still restrained from coming into the open, yet so she smiled a little more to persuade him.

"I don't remember…" Ray finally spoke. "Probably because a lot of tractors often needed mending?"
"Aye an' a half - there's a few of them out here heh, heh," Garstone seemed to buy Ray's story, "but what about when they're all working? I mean here you live in this area of about only twenty-odd residents and next to no advertisement for your trade."
"That reminds me, Greg," Leyton cut in "Ask him about…"

Garstone stayed puzzled before eventually clicking on the shape his partner made in the air with her finger. Just like one of those sign-language translators on late-night BBC repeats, she intrigued him with her ever-inventive string of gesticulations.

"Aye, of course, yeah." he cut from his distraction.
"Ask me about what…?" the mechanic enquired, noticing.

He disapproved of people whispering in front of him especially police officers. To Ray they appeared as shifty as crooks when they conversed amongst themselves in his presence.

"Do you have a business logo of some kind Mr Gipton?" asked Garstone, quickly abandoning his furtive discussion with Leyton, "I assumed you may as you've been at it a few years now."
"Call me Ray. Yes, twenty-seven actually - I started out straight from fifth form. Now, sadly this is all I've been able to muster for a company emblem."

He handed them a set of circular stickers; similar to the brightly coloured sort Garstone was once used to getting from the dentist as a child following his bi-annual check -up. Similar with its bright yellow background, the only writing was the title in purple tailed by the '.com' suffix, with a cartoon-like image of a tyre rack underneath.

"Mm, nice..." Leyton nodded looking at the design, "quite like the one my dad used to go to in Norwich."
"Why do you want to go all the way there for?"
"She's from Cambridge, mate." Garstone decided it would be better speaking for her "Was kinda lacking a reputable mechanic down there, so looks like her old fella sought out other places thereabouts."
"When Michael Aspel's quite finished," said Leyton "my point, Ray, is that we noticed something quite interesting at both Mr McMahon's *and* Mr Ecclesby's scenes."
"Well I'm guessing you lot do find a bit to look at normally when it's a murder."
"Hmm, yes, but we aren't used to every single culprit leaving a strange logo etched in the immediate vicinity of the body."
"Here, pal, this what she means."

Garstone passed Ray a pair of photographs of the symbol, one from each scene. The mechanic was short to draw a cursory conclusion, matching the design up with another he knew only too well from his own youth.

"It could indeed be a gift of that fabled Far Right lot." Ray guessed instinctively, "Wouldn't surprise me."
"Didn't you mention something along those lines recently, Greg?" Leyton quietly asked Garstone.

Seeing this scum of all organisations come up in topic caused

Ray's tone to wilt with   emotion once again, though he just fought off crying to discuss his other recurring troubles of late.

"They've given me dirty looks ever since I arrived in the area. They're never too slow to spot a bloke who doesn't fit in."
"Well, as I am sure you're aware, fascist bodies do tend to also pester individuals based on their sexuality, not just race."
"Pestering?! Part of the reason I moved out here was because my garage in Darnall got smashed up."
"I wholly understand why you elected to relocate." Leyton balanced up "though you plus your friend the late Mr McMahon, both being locally-based are possibly vulnerable. The only thing holding this theory back is that yesterday's victim, Mr Ecclesby was, as far as we know… er, straight."
"There's my boy as well."
"Your boy?"
"Robbie. He's not actually my son, just this young lad who helps out here, about three days a week. Not all there - mentally - but still capable of keeping the premises tidier than I could ever. Rob's like a son to me. I wish I could have him here all the time. I would as well if I got my way."

With this, both detectives simultaneously rolled an eye towards one another as if this reminded them of someone familiar.

5

DEADLY EXPRESSIONS

(i)

The noise of earsplitting disco music had been audible from the lip of the city centre, some two and a half miles away since mid afternoon. A notorious twice-yearly event, the Meadowhall fairground was in the last week of its autumnal stop proving more of an attraction nowadays than the demolition of the twin cooling towers three years before. The masses spilling through the entry gates by teatime bore the usual average age of 15. Very few people could be heard clearly in the disorientating amalgam of coloured lights and colossal refrigerator-sized speakers, set barely feet apart.

That said, it failed to prevent certain individuals from sticking out like sore thumbs: for instance, the lone young man reluctant to vacate his seat on McCrady's Mighty Wagons, leaving a fast-mounting queue for the £2-per-turn attraction waiting.

"Come on, Rob," urged Craig, the attendant who seemed to be used to this particular customer's visits. "I'm sure you've got the right money for another go but these guys need their turn sometime."
"You said I could stay on for another go." the lone figure inside the gondola argued, refusing to budge from his seat.

"Hey, what about you come back in about quarter an hour's time? Promise you it'll be on me" He offered, waiting again for Robbie to respond "Don't be all day mate; this lot are growing impatient,"

Grudgingly, Robbie Draycott emerged from the car to a chorus of derisory ridicule and jeering from the teenage throng awaiting their go, which as normal got to him, making him feel his place in society was below theirs.

"Oi, you lot, that's it, if you still want your go on this ride." Craig reminded them of his favourite customer's disability. "Not his fault he's like that, is it?"
"His fault he's around here though," one of the youths scathingly commented "How come he ain't locked up like all the other psychos are?"
"Don't tempt me."

Craig warned the offending Chav at the front of the line but Robbie wasn't there any more to hear this gent speak in his defence. Though not quite reduced to tears, he still felt emotionally struck by the prejudices of this shallow society and had to get away from the scene. He tried to hold himself from taking it to heart, but this posed a challenge, seen as no typical human actually wore a board, displaying the caption '*I am only kidding*' down it.

Robbie plastered his focus on the spectra of lights enshrouding the countless attractions, something that always seemed to eventually phase existing demons out from his mind, at least temporarily. Sadly it didn't work on the other sudden voice that took him by surprise.

"Hello Robbie."
He turned round to see the figure of a tall and majestically built woman standing right by him. One that matched the exact outline of DI Joanne Leyton,.

"Hi….how are you?"

"Very well. Not causing trouble are we now?"

"I'm causing trouble, what makes you think I'd do that?"

"Oh, nothing, I was just wondering what was going on at the wheel there. Not trying to sneak on without paying were you, you little rascal?"

"He wouldn't let me have another go. Told me I had to come back in half an hour and it would be free"

"Well everyone else needs their turn too. Hey, as you said, you've been promised a free ride in reward for your patience."

She beckoned him to turn himself and his mind away from the ride that had ruled his evening till now. Putting on the old mum-to-a-naughty-kid act, she marched him tightly along till he was out of view of the wheel. By now Robbie didn't mind anymore, happily engaged in conversation.

"So what else has Robbie been on, tonight?"

"Went on Wild Mouse." he pointed her to the turquoise/ orange rollercoaster structure towering behind her. "Spins round when you go on it, it does. Went on it three times."

"You brave boy!" she patted him on the shoulder, "I couldn't even stomach that horrid thing once."

"Been on the Waltzer also- that was great. That goes round really fast, that."

Leyton watched The Disco Ripper accelerate to full rpm, the cars being rotated not only by their masochistic clientele but also by the two attendants, leaping on and off the platform alternately. Robbie scared her, three times more by telling her how the safety bars on this ride were held in place by the passengers themselves, as opposed to locked automatically.

"I'm going on the Enterprise next. I haven't been on it."

Leyton shrunk at the idea of Robbie being spun upside down

inside a harness-less gondola, but at the same time amazed he'd fearlessly board such a thing, its nature so reminiscent of the deadly ride that had nearly ended his life.

"So you prefer rides that just go round and round, I assume... er, *Rob*? Rob what's up?"

The youngster's grin had dropped behind expression matching that of someone finding himself cornered by the Bogeyman. Silenced, along with his petrified gaze Robbie began to back away from her, first slowly then slightly quicker.

"Rob. Come on love, tell me, what's troubling you?"
Leyton vainly coaxed him as he turned and began to walk away, whimpering indecipherably, ignoring her completely.
"Robbie, it's okay, whatever it is, jus..."

Then as if someone else appeared to be stood in front of him, in Leyton's place, Robbie accelerated into a demented dash across the centre of the fair. Scattering the visitors, like a ride car come off its mountings the chaos was significantly comparable as adults and kids alike dived aside, those of the two-five-year-old range caught totally off guard.

"It's... it's ok...   Robbi... Oh god..."

She was already fifty feet into her pursuit as she reached for her mobile, and bashed at the buttons, hoping she would get the right number without looking. Talking into the receiver while running at 20mph through an overcrowded fairground, *while* trying not to instigate the same carnage as Robbie was a tall contest. She tried to keep the call to Garstone as brief, but audible as possible although that was a miracle alone with her style of running.

"Greg, if you've actually bothered having your trip to the fair tonight, can I borrow you a minute - a certain friend has gone a bit er…*funny*."

Leyton sensed an understatement had been made on her part as Robbie, ahead ploughed through the throngs like a runaway bull. Awaiting a reply from Garstone, she still had less problems than expected pursuing the runaway through the fairground, as the hurriedly parting crowds, paved her trail for her. A tirade of abuse gradually took form as she flayed her way across the unyielding remainder; only three magic words able to put these hostile obstructers in their place.

"Move! Police officer!" she bellowed haphazardly, clutching her mobile against her face, as an imaginary radio. *"Greg, come on…. Get out of that ca….*oh no…."

A large crashing sent her attention off left, round towards the duck stall. The crumbling canopy had just landed to rest as she got to the scene, spilt water and yellow plastic ducks clarifying that someone had indeed finished their escape rather painfully.

"Oh, Robbie. Robbie…. Robbie…. Robbie…"

Leyton chorused as she lay back in her chair in the interview room, trying to place aside her embarrassment at seeing this particular figure in the seat normally reserved for crooks. Robbie cowered in his chair, a total wreck not well aided by the deep water he believed himself now in. Stuck for other sympathetic words left, having bled the dictionary dry she rocked forward onto the edge of the table shaking her head.

"*So-o-o* what are we going to do, eh?"
"They're going to take my photo aren't they?" Robbie stammered, atremble "Going to make me give them my fingerprints, and then they're going to lock me up."

"Hopefully, it won't come to that, for the foreseeable future."

"What, I'm not under arrest then?"

"Not for the little disaster at the fairground – the girl on the stall was convinced you were not a regular troublemaker. You didn't really break much - at least nothing in there, eh?"

Leyton playfully prodded him on the right arm to interpret that.

"Why am I here then?" Robbie didn't seem convinced of his innocence.

"We need to talk again a bit. Don't worry, darling, you *are* going home but while waiting for your lift, why don't you tell me where you got that gigantic 'whatever-it-is' down the side of your face there?"

"I thought you said I was OK,"

"I'm sure you are, but can I just look at it for a second? I promise I won't touch."

With Robbie's cautious co- operation, she lifted the side of his hair to examine the faded but still ominous stitch line. It was purely horrible - from his left ear all the way down to the chin, it grew approximately three times the size of what she'd first expected, dividing his head practically in two.

"Robbie, you can not seriously expect me to accept that *this* was an accident! "

"Not an accident! " Robbie suddenly blurted loudly. "No accident, no!"

"It was deliberate, is that what you are trying to say?"

"He pushed me, the man did."

"Man? What man? Craig, the 'wheel' bloke, was that him? Superintendent Hargreaves? Ray? Has he done something to you?"

"No, leave Ray alone, it wasn't him... wasn't him pushing me."

"You've run that past me already. Pushed you off *what*?"

"Pushed me, pushed me very fast… round and round. That's what he said. *Round and round*! He wo-ouldn't sto-op-p!"

Robbie's explosion dissolved into tears all over the table. Having waited till he'd stopped pounding his hands, Leyton threw her chair next to his and put her arm around him, tight. Comforting her distraught friend, she couldn't escape the grasp of slightly familiar words on her shoulder right now: '*Round and round*' for instance. The third time in two days that this small expression had popped up yet like the symbol, she could still not place a marker on its significance.

(Now on top of all this he mentions being pushed. But by who, for Christ's sake?!) Robbie's mum had taken her right through the tale, - rather vividly too - only yesterday, but that was surely in referral to the original injury. Not this fearsome laceration newly arrived overnight. (*That could be it.*) Leyton wondered whether Robbie knew if they were talking about the same one - she ought to have known that any damage on the clarity factor might spark confusion.

Three people's names continually rose to mind, but no direct answer came from the gibbering heap bawling into the table, alongside. Or that scar. (*How can he get it from going 'round and round'- that must be one evil serving of g-forces he was subjected to.*) This time of night, all escaped her mind; she was supposed to have been off duty at five-thirty as it was. Here at quarter past ten, she'd usually be past caring till rising from the sheets next morning, were it anyone other than Robbie Draycott in front of her right now.

Thompson called in to pick up Robbie up for a 'lift' that awaited him. Leyton saw him to the door, but stayed in the room till this ill-connecting link, she found tricky to splice back came at least halfway to her again. Both the two scars had to stay in front of her eyes - no photo of the fresher smart probably existed yet but alongside the closed one of seven years back, the differences in profile separated them by their causes.

(ii)

As Leyton stood on the tiled step of the HQ's vast reception doorway, merely half an hour later she felt it getting to her even more than she herself first felt. One person little known for crying, this evening together with Robbie had tested her to the brink and now she felt it filling up inside like a lavatory cistern. The initial sniffle came, just about contained from everyone, except the friendly young North-Eastern gent stood at her immediate right.

"If you want to weep a little, I'm not gonna look." Garstone spoke, facing guiltily to the other side. "But I've got a way better place in mind to drown your sorrows… and am taking you there, right this instant."
"Oh, are you indeed?"
"If you forget, Jo, your orders end outside the station door. So my orders are 'pub' and 'now'! Come on, Leroy's waiting."

Resigned to having little say in this extra-curricular requirement, Leyton shrugged and stepped into the passenger side. From closing the door and fastening her belt, Leyton never once craned back at the station's walls behind, just enjoying another orange/silver light display scrolling by, that often cured her daily depressions. Only Garstone could keep that particular button inside Joanne Leyton's head held down, shame he ruined it as he arrived at his little side space off West Street quicker than expected.

"Come on, out you get."

"Are we supposed to be here already?"

"Aye, you were that far 'away' you didn't notice."

"Ok, Greg, I remember, it's *just up here round the corner then about two hours walk, on the right, cross at the lights.*"

"Y' see, you can pick up when you try, though you've got the pub wrong."

Emerging into the brightly floodlit world of West Street, she was almost lost by Garstone's ramblings again, only to be clocked right round to her left. The blue-lit lettering above hardly had time to register as 'McGanlon's before his ivory-sleeved hand thrust open the tinted double doors, introducing Leyton to a world she had forgotten over the last seventy-two hours - a social life.

McGanlon's Merry Wine Lodge was the regular after-duty watering hole they made pilgrimage to. Discovered on Garstone's first Monday night out with the Midelson gang last year, the Irish-backed bar served food till late, all seven days though on the flip side it was amongst the most driver-unfriendly venues in Sheffield. Garstone had christened a space off the end of Westfield Terrace officially his. Concealed by the outer signage scheme, the intern of the pub had a Tardis-like vastness with a misty red-lit tint that blended against the mahogany playing hell with most visiting peoples' eyes struggling to adapt.

"I see you 'just managed' to find a seat." Garstone congratulated the solitary customer perched at one of the high tables.

"What happened in here then? Drink prices trebled overnight or something?"

"It might be to do with who one of the other customers is,"

Armitage tipped his head at a small table near the bandit, over which a charcoal wax anorak was untidily draped. (*Whose is that*

96

I wonder?) Leyton instantly recognised the coat. She crept over and lifted it away by the collar to find the designer label on the lining, just about making out the 'Bandell & Abbott's' wordage, when the opening of a door behind made her drop it and back away.

"Find it interesting do you, D.I. Leyton?"

She whirled round, swiftly to confirm the owner and immediately fished for her best excuse, hoping that DCS Hargreaves might just buy it.

"Just thought you might like it hanging up."
"No thanks, I like to keep it where I can see it. Just as well, eh?"
"Whatever. Anyway, instead of sitting over here by yourself, why don't you join the boys and me over here?"
"Sorry, Leyton, but as you might have noticed, I have a paper lying on the table here, with its page sat wide open on yesterday's United game. Take a hint?" A point of finger directing her back towards the other table, more or less settled the picture.
"Suit yourself, you miserable git!"

She signed herself out of yet another less-than-friendly conversation, but not silently enough to be unheard. Her DCS fumed momentarily, wishing they had still been on the job at that moment, a sought-after insubordination charge against her now an opportunity cruelly lost.

"You haven't invited him over, have you?" Garstone dreaded.
"I tried, knowing exactly what the response would be," Leyton replied passively.
"You know, I'm surprised you keep asking, you stupid tart!" Hargreaves cawed from his perch "This ain't a chuffing Cambridge Uni' common room you're in now, duck."

"Well I'd hardly expect you to be there if it was, sir, would I?"
"Leave it," Garstone poked her, "Look, he's over there, your friends are right here. Now shut up and choose something before we die of starvation."

Harangued by his nagging persistence, she picked up the plastic menu sheet, at least smiling in the awareness she could choose without checking her watch for once. A recently introduced policy that the pub's 5.99 list applied through till ten on weeknights allowed them to choose from Cheeseburger Champion, Tickled Rib Rack, Fairy CodMother, Big Bangers and Mighty Mash, or Cajun Fighter, and then between variably miniscule portions of chips or over-heaped watercress salad as the small print designated.

The menu enthralled Leyton so much usually it delayed her enough for the boys to be already eating by the time she'd chosen: however, turning out in a downset mood on occasions saw her fail to absorb it. Tonight they were just a load of fancily-labelled dishes, on a fancily-coloured menu… purchased from a fancily-named supermarket chain.

"That got her quiet, didn't it?" Armitage levelled with his other DC, then completely spoiled it again "So now then, ma'am, what's this I hear about you crying outside the station?"
"I can't keep my mind off Robbie, particularly on the gravity of tonight."
"Well I know this'll defeat the point of us being here but, er…better out than in."

While she took a moment getting her words right, as well as her food, Garstone filled Armitage in on the matter and what he'd learned regarding the events that had apparently messed up Robbie's life long before.

"Is that why he's like, 'not all there'?" the DC guessed emptily.
"The creatures who pushed him off a swing at thirteen suit that one more aptly."
"Pushed off?!" Garstone found something horribly chilling in Leyton's revelation "You said nothing' about that before. Still it puts me a wager on your next word."
"I could pick from many. At least I found out how 'Round and round' comes into it."
"Didn't that one come from the old lass up Green Oak?" Armitage suddenly found bells ringing.
"Precisely, Leroy. And that boy is scared - the murder at Dore clearly evoked too many personal traumas. This particular phrase is becoming a curse, so it seems."

Leyton felt a substantial weight quickly fall from her back, and allowed for a sip of her House White, with the comfort. She couldn't help noticing that Hargreaves was looking in her direction once again, though the octagonal lenses miraculously never shattered from their wearer's black-eyeballed ugliness. Looking down into her wine momentarily, as if pretending not to notice she took a second sip before glancing left. Hargreaves now had his eyes re-attached to the pages of his Daily Mail like glue. Noticing Armitage reading this surplus anxiety, she grabbed her next set of words before he or Garstone had chance.

"So I can rightly assume *you've* spotted Robbie's new 'decorations' then, Leroy?"
"Aye, I heard summat. Has he been up to talking about it?"
"In little bits. The line 'he pushed me' was a well repeated lyric in his tune tonight."
"That's probably it then," Garstone sped up the answer for Armitage, "Hardly any point asking beyond that, eh?"
"While I appreciate your observance as well, Greg, you might have noticed the total absence of stitching in the new scar."
"Wasn't actually sayin' he got it like, yesterday or somethin' -

could have had the stitches out again."

As she took another silent practice at the unpronounceable German name on the wine whilst nodding, Garstone felt like he was beginning to sense somewhere in Leyton's evaluation, how his judgement had also played parts. (The *attack happened just yesterday...no wait on it was about a year ago, the Draycott kid was attacked by a swing wielding nut... no hold on he was pushed.) No*, he'd instead worsened a two-way miscommunication that was to see her fire another ball back in his direction.

"Neither park sits within walls, just large vast fields -I can't begin to figure where he would have picked up the newer wound by accident."
"Yeah, but *where* does all this about him being attacked come from?!" he cautiously probed "No disrespect, but is there any chance of squeezing a few straight words from him, now he's chilled out?"
"Yes, hopefully tomorrow, during a chat at home with him and his wonderful mum."

Both DCs seemed confused by Leyton's convoluted tales as her sense of perseverance became increasingly all over the place, still making next-to-no sense with this story. One thing that made no difference was that last bit Garstone had just heard.

"You let him go?!"

Garstone believed this was either his DI seriously losing the plot, or feeling uncomfortable about detaining Robbie any longer at the time with Hargreaves listening in the office next door, neither much better than the other.

"Ma'am, if someone's wanting another pop at that kid from

where he last left it, we need to keep him around."

"No charges have been pressed; also he was quiet as a mouse after his half-hour cooling off time. If all that fails to convince, he even told me to take care of myself on his way...on his way ...out." She fixed both eyes in a puzzled stare at that table once more. "Hargrea..."

"I told you," Garstone warned her, forcefully "don't keep looking at him."

"I wouldn't be if he was there to look at."

Hargreaves's chair sat vacant, the paper folded far-from-neatly in two and pinned down by his half empty glass. This largely baffled all the three detectives - the DCS was known to perform untimely disappearing acts but rarely in front of Leyton, much as she wished he'd perform them more. It just felt like he'd been an unwelcome mirage, all evening to them.

"Reckon he's just gone for a wazz?" Armitage commented, totally off-cuff.

"Hardly, unless he's so possessive of his coat, he takes it and hangs it over the urinal. With a bit of luck it will drop straight into the deadly yellow."

"Ey, I'd like to see how many times that needs to go through the wash."

Perplexed by Leyton's knowledge of a men's lavatory Armitage marginally kept it contained, for the joke. Garstone however had gone to see, but on finding the men's cubicles completely bereft of any occupants decided to poke his head round the fire exit. A pair of tail lights could be seen turning away at the bottom.

"Can I help you, mate?" asked a voice that was thankfully too young to be owned by Hargreaves but still quite demanding of the DC's business.

"Nah, nothing'...." Garstone knew that wouldn't justify his unpermitted use of the fire door to Gavin, the young student barman. "Hey was there another guy came out through here just now? Got into a car."

"Yeah, think that was him, just went down that way," Gavin seemed a little more relaxed by Garstone's nature, "Big old bloke in a Volvo. Not nicking it was he?"

"No, no... just, you know...just wondering....oh never mind."

He backed away inside again, letting him close the door, and returned to the company.

"Seems he's left the building," Garstone let out a suggesting chuckle.

"That settled," Leyton finished her glass, "is there any more in that bottle?"

"I'd think so," Armitage presented the wine from the seat where he had hidden it, attempting his best French accent "*Let ze waiter pour for you, madame.*"

"Oh, you little monkey!" she watched as he tipped it completely on end, filling the glass to the top, plus a little further "I should have known why you were so keen."

The laughter nearly turned Leyton fully to her senses, as the wine now turned to champagne for all three of them. Trying for a face of relaxation, she slowly won the lads over until they were engrossed in a three-way discussion about lighter issues of the day. As the banter rolled in thick and fast, the mood finally pitched high enough to keep either DC from making sure she wasn't having one of her sneaky revisits to that 'other world' of hers, lately created.

Hiding her face frequently with another full glass, Garstone and Armitage would have been right to assume Leyton was still attempting to bottle her gremlins, as if they had even spent the nightime spying through her window.

102

These worries indeed went on to claw at her, practically all night, save for the brief period of 4.30-6.15 am after which trying to grab further minutes sleep seemed useless, at which point she finally gave in, diving for the bathroom. Sticking to everything boiling hot, from shower water almost fully in the red, to coffee drunk straight from pouring, everything to keep her awake till the turn of evening had to be considered, including three entire bowlfuls of *All Bran* this morning instead of two. Hoping a certain someone else was also awake by this time, she casually reached for her cordless.

"Hello, boy wonder, are you up and raring to go?"
"*You* phoning *me* first thing in the morning?" Garstone sounded as cheery and alert as usual if not unsurprised, "That's a new one."
"I was just wondering what activities you have lined up this morning, Greg, if any."
"Heh heh heh, is that an offer by any chance?"
"Might have been, had that wine last night proved a higher volume than on the label. I was wondering if there's anything I or *we* can get straight off to - even if it's just a stupid little littering offence, it'll be sufficient right now."
"Are you keen or what? You've slept well to come up with one like this."
"Actually I didn't. I'm just interested in pursuing any situation that'll keep me out of the station for the morning, or preferably the day."
"What's up- you not trying to give Hargreaves a wide berth again are you?"

(When has she not?) It didn't elude Garstone that if 'Satan's Superintendent' neglected to inflict his trident on Leyton's tyres last night, he obviously had something equally vindictive lined up for her today instead. Hopefully missing the sight of her face

for a few hours would enable Hargreaves to forget which mouldy lunch item he intended for her drawer - as by which time he'd be too fully engrossed in matters of the morning anyway. Either way, any person sneaking out through a restaurant fire exit in full view of other police officers, automatically filed in Joanne Dawn Leyton's conscience as suspicious.

"On the subject of wide berths," Leyton finally ended her silent moment of worry "where are you now?"
"Look outside your window. Best be quick, I'm on a bus lane here."
"So you have come round to make sure I'm not worrying again, have you?"
"If you *are still* worrying - I'd understand it right now. You're still not as worried as Robbie Draycott's mum is this morning."
"I think I know that already."
"I'll try that again, in English. He's gone missing."
"WHAT?!"
"Yep, near his house."
"Greg, stay right where you are! Keep the engine running!"

6

OLD SWINGERS AND DEAD RINGERS

(i)

Very few, if not in fact no individual being at all, could replicate the speed at which Leyton dressed then tore down the steps into Garstone's waiting Vectra this particular morning. However, even a merest utterance of their current star witness Robbie Draycott's name was enough to make her sit up in her bed, let alone when paired with the word 'missing'.

Thinking about his sickening new stripe, Leyton remembered her releasing Robbie from custody as going down well with her two colleagues last night; was she now having the biggest regret over both of them come this morning?

"Before you ask, info's a bit basic." advised Garstone. "She was in a treat of a state, her mum you know."
"Did you get anything out of her?"
"Yes - 'big chap and a mate' got out of a car, landed right on him. Just called the kid everything under the sun then shut him inside the boot."
"Could always be some bigger sibling, Danny Bennington deliberately never warned us of."
"I'd crap myself at the age-gaps in his family, then - this '*chap*' was about fifty-odd."
"Erm…really?"

Leyton hadn't actually got round to fingering local bigots, but it stayed relevant, though someone old enough to be his dad was less than she expected. (Christ *I can understand how Robbie, the way he is, would have become a sitting paedophile target)*

"Good morning boys."

She cut off the chat as a marked unit broke in from the ring road, with a very familiar red Ford Focus in tow. Both pulled across right in front of her, diving right onto the kerb outside Aizlewood's Mill. Swinging his door wide into the passing traffic as usual Armitage bounded over, arms waving at them like a railway signal in gale force winds.

"Ey' ma'am, you mind telling me where the heck you're going?" Armitage queried as she lowered the window.
"I believed we were all bound for the Draycott residence."
"Eh? What do you want wi' up there?"
"Our friend Robbie's done a vanishing act - I just merely assume that's why you're tearing it up through town as well."
"You'll be the one doing that in a second, ma'am," said PC Hall, joining them. "Hargreaves needs us up Totley, fast."
"Probably he means just me, Chris.... that or everyone else apart from myself."
"Can't say anything more, just you've got your work cut out for you, today."

Leyton took that look at Garstone again.

"You want to go with Lee?" her other DC grasped the hint, "I'll see to this Robbie business."

Without a time to argue, Leyton piled into the Focus and her new chauffeur, having applied the blue light to his roof tore off like a spacefighter in a sci-fi movie, Hall's vehicle leading the way.

The ten-minute flight, to the end of Totley village seemed like ten hours to her as she used freedom from the wheel as excuse

106

for further dis-attachment, though Armitage was also ready to stick his over-attentive nose in as usual.

Restraining him from an unadvisable trip into Leyton's light fantastic-isms, was his own calculator-like appraisal of this long-driven route and the game he loved to play to himself along it. Splitting into sectors like a grand prix lap, the Sheffield centre to Totley trek happened on a timetable. (*Moorfoot - Abbeydale picture house, 2.5 mins, there to Millhouses - 3,Millhouses to Beauchief ...23.75 seconds, record fastest*). Often best achieved without his disapproving DI riding shotgun, Armitage rarely allowed time to appreciate the ever-changing image of Abbeydale Road that he had often watched from the window of his dad's Triumph Dolomite, twenty five years before.

There were a darn sight less boarded up shop fronts in the eighties than here in the 'twenty-tens'. Businesses visibly expanded outside the city more than in it just recently, contrastable with the recession-ravaged 'wasteland' he'd normally glimpsed from most traffic crossings, whenever a stop for the red offered him such seconds. Dore wasn't in the healthiest of sight today either with the Chrysler showroom and garden centre gone amongst others, leaving an ugly looking car park in its place.

Running short on things to speak about, (most of which he'd borrowed from his father) reality again had to destroy his retrospective reflections, if not solely for the need of defying that squint-eyed look from Leyton, once more.

"Were me ears playing tricks on me then, ma'am, or did I just hear that bleedin' kid's name mentioned again?" He listened as Leyton reeled off the shocking news,
"Eh? You're kidding.... outside his own chuffin' place? What sort of heartless bastard goes doing stuff like that? Talked to

Danny, yet?"

"Not yet but we won't give him a completely wide berth over it."

"Aye, ought to keep him well in the loop. You know what his type are like, hitting on people with problems."

Armitage's language clearly made Leyton flinch. Describing a person like Robbie that way, bordered hardly more legal than 'Robbie the Retard'. Reacting to her 'I thought you knew better than that' look, he shifted his discussion onto their other person of interest.

'Ey, you don't reckon it were that Ray bloke calling round to pick him up?"

"Robbie always walks to work. He's a very fit lad - more to the point he was arriving back from his morning jog when these two barbarians swooped."

"How far from his house, were he?"

"Literally about fifteen feet from the door. I can't name any faces at this moment, but all the same I'd still prefer to think it was random."

(*Whenever some burly stranger ambushes an innocent and vulnerable lad outside his own home in the small hours of the morning then piles him into the back of a car like a bag of potatoes, it's got to be personal.*)

"Hey you don't reckon someone's got a grudge?" Armitage probed quite accurately into Leyton's not-so-silent mind.

"On Robbie, what you do mean?" Leyton sounded aghast that Armitage could dream such a thing up. "How would Robbie Draycott deserve to be on *anyone*'s hit list?"

"Never took liberties with anyone, has he? No one got a score to settle?"

"A score …with *Robbie*? I can hardly see that likely, Leroy, but regarding liberties, someone has taken the most appalling one

imaginable - it sickens even hardy officers like me. Honestly."
"I were just thinking- me dad always told me, his sort can have skeletons in their cupboard like anyone other."

(...and some probably just end up that way) Leyton felt like quoting her partners probable forthcomings *(and yes, for all we know Robbie could have ended up in the state he is through worrying about them finally falling out, one day when someone opens the door.)*

"Trust me, whatever Robbie Draycott's done in the past is forgiven, from my perspective." She could read his next words as if a flashing red warning light had come on.

The weary conversation stretched a further eternity of minutes, becoming almost a game of football with the names Robbie and Danny being kicked to and fro but no goals looking to be scored anytime yet. Eventually, a sea of lights, at the distant end of Baslow Road blew the whistle on this already frustrating game.

Slowing on a nudge from Leyton, Armitage's vehicle was immediately swarmed as if some already knew who had the other seat in Armitage's car this morning.

"Morning, ma'am, glad you finally made it," PC Thompson welcomed her.
"Only because of someone bumping into us in town." she winked at Armitage as he slammed the door in his trademark demeanour. "So, what have we got today then?"
"Well I don't know about you, but the Harvester's Plough has taken delivery of a new garden hammock overnight."

Leyton turned round to Armitage, hoping he could translate PC Thompson's long-winded description of whatever awaited, as the vast hordes of blue, white and bright yellow –clad personnel broke aside to grace her arrival.

The solid wall of people, encircling the lawn outside the old pub seemed determined to remain solidly put. In contrast to her arrival at Dore in Wednesday, only a vague nodding of reverence to Sheffield's most popular detective appeared affordable with the severity of this latest incident. She noticed the chains of both outer swings slewed together, so was a little led by Thompson's comment.

"Okay boys, let's see this new addition to the furniture then."

The mostly-hooded crowd parted in half like a theatre curtain allowing Leyton into the gap, though she was soon beginning to wish she had requested different. Lying in front of her, though some two feet off the ground the figure cloaked in a dark burgundy zip jacket could have been a stuffed mannequin for all they knew, given its contortion.

Suspended by the chains of the outer swings, the ensnared body was bent almost into a full banana shaped posture, twisted enough that she found herself looking straight into his two wide-open yet totally lifeless eyes, bulging from a face that peeped out of the balaclava of coiled rope.

"Bloody 'ell, how's he managed to do that?" Armitage feebly hid his difficulty in stomaching the macabre find himself.
"I understand how the word 'hammock' enters into the equation."

Leyton drew his attention to things more important still as she pointed at the centre of the corpses' trunk, which was about half a foot closer to the floor without a central swing to support it.

"You know, ma'am." Armitage looked down at the floor, as he talked "I don't know which is the most sickening I've heard this morning; Robbie or this."

(Well, preying on a mentally ill 20-year-old man who can't even hurt a fly is as low as it gets itself, but bumping someone off in such a way as this...)

'Pure' and 'Evil' were normally two regular completions for the line but for Leyton, a woman of many a word, '*Cunning* and '*genius*' slowly overtook to come first capturing the body and all its trimmings as one package. Everything appeared thought out with this deed, down to the last detail. If be the same felon, he had taken plenty of lessons home from his Dore and Green Oak escapades, though she could tell he'd opted to model mostly on the former. Knowing to expect a modern wooden swing here, with rope as opposed to a chain, one thing was bursting with certainty; the murderer had done his extra homework overnight, either bypassing the location on leaving Green Oak yesterday or having visited the place with his fantasises in view, five-six weeks beforehand.

The colourless head indicated a minimum of four hours without air, about identical to Roy Ecclesby's state on his discovery. She half-knelt to look at his clothes. Knowing to expect them of the same barely-missed-by-explosion condition as either his or Mr McMahon's outer garb, there were fewer significant rips down the front, but occasional encounters with pub grass and pavement grit where he'd been hauled across from the car weighed heavily on the mutilation quota.

"I thought his top were burgundy not red." Armitage moaned.
"When you bump someone off at six o'clock in the morning with only the orange of streetlights to guide your crime, red and purple both show up more or less the same."
"Like grey-ish red, you mean? That?"
"Yes. Unfortunately, what might slow us up this time is the

chance that he forgot to leave his familiar trade-mark behind."
"Shall I have a couple of lads check around the frame, just in
case there's summat?"
"Yes, go for it. There's every chance they could've just stuck it
quickly on with a marker somewhere."

She turned back to the crowd stood flocked over the deceased.
Trying to see what was happening, she was ignorantly walled out
by the analysts and Thompson's inaudible gabbling from
somewhere there within.

"I say, is there a possibility I can actually see my latest body
without all of you standing in the way?"
"No, ma'am, sorry," said Pathologist Stubbs, "due to the body's
vulnerable posture we need to stabilise it centrally."
"I'd think asking nicely inside for one of their chairs should sort
the problem."
"They've only got children's seats available that slide under -
they're nowhere near the height we require."
"Get a bloody cushion then!" Leyton ranted, quite fed up of the
petty arguing on top of their incompetence.
"Ma'am, here!" called Thompson, invisibly from round from the
side.

Leyton jumped along to find he'd forged her gangway, although
he had something other than the dead man to aim her at.

"Lord, it must have been something intriguing, Will to draw you
into staring."
"You'll be the first to agree, I guarantee it."

The PC invited her to see a familiar round shape, carved halfway
up the post.

"If it is what I think, yet again, I'm familiar but fascinated still, as

to who or why."
"There's a visible difference, if you look from closer perspective.

(*Hmm, yes he's missed a little bit.*) She noticed an anomaly regarding its precision here. The newly immortal icon had not been fully completed this time - the circle was etched thrice as before but now only half an arrow, the left part visually omitted. Though proof that it had been attempted rested, the hurried effort told Leyton little new about the killer. She spoke it out loud to herself but Thompson was standing too close to miss it, especially her passing reference to weapon detail.

"We can't confirm the type of instrument used," Thompson quibbled.
"It's either a Stanley, or another knife of that type. I haven't time to… argue." She calmed down as noticing Armitage was looking, from his place amongst the 'body' party. "Yes, Leroy?"
"Better come check this out." Her friend seemed discreetly excited.

Leyton joined him as the body was now rolled fully over, thanks to the suggested aid of two chairs borrowed from inside the pub. She wasn't too flattered to find her men had positioned them with the back nearer but Armitage was in before she could think.

"Look," he pointed closely to the body's facial regions. "Notice something?"
"Erm yes, so I appear to be looking at man of some forty or so years of age, caucas..."
"I mean *not* see something, see something that's, like 'not there', sorry."
"Well his eyes are still open this time...oh *hello-o!*"

Her scrutiny became attracted to the central region of the man's face, closer examination revealing a nude upper lip here. This

113

third murder was a *first* amongst the set, Leyton not yet expecting the killer to be targeting the clean-shaven half of society. Nonetheless, she seemed satisfied at last, standing up with a returned grin towards Armitage, which had to be defended as he walked straight over.

"It looks like moustaches are going to come off the manifesto now." she showed him the face, to translate, also referring back to it for herself. "There's still the red - well *burgundy* - sweatshirt so it's not been a total waste. (We do now have *a* lead.)"
"Ey up, where they going?"

Armitage noticed a familiar uniformed unit pulling up by on the street. PC Islington leant out of the window. Both detectives galloped over, Leyton obviously noting they sought her.

"D.I Leyton!   Where have you been?" Islington sounded very hasty, "They're all waiting for you! BMX track, down behind the old Tec'!"
"Just what exactly are they up to at a stunt course when there's a murder to solve!?"
"You mean no one's told you yet?"
"Told me what, may I ask? Leyton demanded, quite annoyed.

(ii)

Armitage and Leyton both dived into the back of the car, without bothering to hear what 'what' or 'it' were exactly, but the officer driving felt they were tuned into the way the wind was blowing. The half minute long escort, down the gratuitously pot-holed Totley Hall Lane left Leyton next to no time to picture the situation that had attracted half of her most vital team to meandering around a public sports field. Only something of equally dramatic criminal magnitude justified this unheard-of abandonment in duty.

She would see it right now as the officer pulled up at the open gateway, not that a gate of any description remained in situ any longer between the crumbling posts. This elongated grassland, backing off an upmarket housing estate where University buildings once towered, was decorated with the same amenities as Green Oak and Dore but most attraction was around the mound straight down from her. The biking circuit, itself badly in disrepair since 2006 took some recognition with its overgrowth but Islington hadn't the spare time.

"You'd better hop out here ma'am," he advised "there's too much traffic in, already."
"Er, right, okay," Leyton pretended not to sound awkward "I think I can see where I'm needed."

The impenetrable dome of personnel swarming the embankments sent Leyton straight to her scene, her eyes growing their own pair of legs that walked way in front of the rest of her. Dodging through the new car park that had been created for the morning, Leyton could not help but be diverted by the recently-built play area to the right; not a soul surrounded that, living or dead. The lone swing, hanging vacantly within its wooden frame, cut a spooky silhouette in the lingering fog swallowing the bottom of the field. It did not feel that new to her but from the collection of pine climbing apparatus and other recreational shapes, a new dimension had already formed.

She had seen golden opportunities shunned frequently at the last second, but rarely when the ultimately desired time and place beckoned. Perhaps the culprit's luck ran out when he ran out from that pub garden. Could this be *he*, lying here - the victim of an impromptu vigilante trap? Enough people in Sheffield knew of the first two attacks already, front-page fodder on both the Star and national papers. Either Mr McMahon or Ecclesby may have a friend or relative with the temerity to take the law into their own hands. Or was it circumstantial meandering, maybe just one more nightly alcohol poisoning statistic adding onto Britain's many?

The mundane actuality arose as the equally dreary weekday weather came, along with another anti-climactic find. Craning her eyes round to see the line of redundant telegraph poles on the hill above Strawberry Lea Lane, this vision came to her regularly, killing any glimmer of brilliance that rescued grey landscapes back to green.

Solving a case outside the current sequential trend didn't exactly bode for momentum but Leyton had to remain committed. Her appearance still didn't improve her collaborators' manners, she herself having to make separate taps on each shoulder for attention.

"I'd better warn you, ma'am," advised the forensic stood nearest "it's not a pretty sight."
"Not much is in this job." she supplemented her own agreement.

The four officers in the centre rose to their feet like a flowering bud in summer, leaving the eager bee that was Joanne Leyton to reach pollen more bloody than the average insect was used to. She took up the position she had just relieved them from, hunching round the dirtied red/brown heap barely resembling a human body. Shuffling the sheet away, a bloodied face gazed up while a darkening shade discoloured the sand below him.

Letting one of the officers move the head back a very tiny way, she pulled the collar away, immediately to find a grisly incision round the perimeter of the throat. The dried blood acted like rotted Velcro as lumps came off with a pull, having slowly materialised into the coat.

"I hate to point out the obvious to you here," she greeted them "but it looks like the weapon's something distinctively sharper than rope or chains this time."
"Or his fingernails." Raylesthorpe's lifted the right hand up.

(My, which blackboard did this chap lose a fight with?) Leyton studied the nails, or what remained of them. Long uncut, up to the death they had been forced right off the thumb, index and little fingers, those on the middle and ring digits bent right to the limit. Small traces of blood appeared from most of them, plus sand and slight grit in the index.

Moving on to the left, something that jumped out at her from one side grabbed her throat from the other. Only one nail, the middle finger's was displaced this time but the intact four were painted underneath by an assortment ranging from blood, earth, sand and something blackish-blue under the thumb. She invited Raylesthorpe to see.

"Recognise that colour? Lovely shade, don't you think?"
"Navy, I reckon, ma'am, or darker."

Raylesthorpe, bringing his student-barely-recovered-from-Saturday attitude to the job along with his appallingly un-brushed ginger crop, wasted the standard minutes quibbling the odds on whereabouts the minute strand of fabric had begun its life. Whether from off a police uniform - or one of the many other things she went on to list for the benefit of penetrating his thick ignorant skull - drew Leyton to ultimately hammer down her point.

"My god, it's such a struggle with you lot, isn't it sometimes?"

117

Very unlikely to have registered the 'S' word, Raylesthorpe looked on as the analyst supported it in his hands. His guess was more of overalls than officer's jacket, although Leyton approved of the thought. A hefty abrasion of skin from the thumb down to the wrist was also a telling sign - the victim must have caught it on the offender's watch as he lost grip with this hand and slipped straight down.

"You said something about it being a guy's overalls, perhaps?" Raylesthorpe interrupted "Could be that mechanic you talked to yesterday... Mr Gibson was it?"
"*Gipton*, you mean? Yes..." Leyton openly recalled.... "His overalls were actually more of the yellow variety,"
"Hmm...he did have a company motif on his chest pocket."
"True..." Leyton kept Raylesthorpe happy with her considerations for a few wavy moments "That was a contrast yes. Nothing to suit the navy blue range, however."

New theories remaining un-dismissed as yet, the badge idea almost settled with her. A logo or crest could often be a sew-on patch, especially if it was a smaller company. (*Nope hold on, that would be wrong - the victim was grabbing at the offender's sleeve - when has a sew-on patch ever been on that part of the jumpsuit?*) She was about to try testing Raylesthorpe again only for him to do just as good a job on her himself.

"Ah, yeah... I think it were a Rolex."
"For crying out loud, Mike!" Leyton nearly exploded "Whatever make, it hardly matters, most of the damn things are sharp in places as it is, but right now it's not what I'm discussing."
"If watches fascinate you, Leyton," a gruff and unfortunately familiar voice boomed into her right ear, "Why don't you invest some of your hard-*un*earned money in one now and again?"

Hargreaves didn't bother holding on for a reply. He walked round in a small circle, casually judging that work on the scene was already progressing before whirling back up to Leyton.

"Still glad you could spare the time. Managed to avoid a lock in last night, eh?"
"Yes, I did actually, so did Leroy and Greg- given that we went at ten past eleven."
"Speaking of whom," Hargreaves looked past her with cold curiosity "You're missing one half of the likely lads at present. What's Garstone's excuse not to be about?"
"Robbie's been abducted! I'm surprised you hadn't been filled on that already, seeing it was reported prior to these incidents. Must say, it's lucky enough that his mum and Greg exchanged numbers when they did, isn't it."
"But not that you sent that useless streak of Geordie piss up there - you'd be the one best suited for scenes not requiring your own personal sick bucket."
"Well excuse me but I needed it more than ever."
"Okay, okay - don't make me do something that I'll get the sack for."

He fished inside his pocket for the lump of filthy tattered mush only he could still recognise as his notebook, obviously reserving his oldest worst kept paper for Leyton's concerns with the hope of not being able to write them down. Quite inevitably, he was none too happy to find his biro still wrote. The Superintendent obviously didn't want to pretend he actually cared about the safety of Leyton's friend, an integral witness as Robbie now was. Still she had to try her best, leaving resentment towards her boss on the backburner.

"So what was he dressed up in, if not something with his name splattered all over the front? (*Would be about right for a half-case like Draycott, wouldn't it.*)"

"Blue fleece zip top, black jogging bottoms, and trainers of some sort too, obviously."

"That's funny. You know, I picked a young chap up matching that description only this morning. Your little friend Draycott doesn't go running, does he?"

"Sometimes, or so I've heard. His mum said..."

"'Yes', or 'no' would have been enough. Anyway, I haven't had time to take this chap in yet, so if you want to have a word I'll keep 'Mr Blobby' meanwhile occupied."

Upholding his usual policy on unwarranted chatter, the DCS backed away disinterested. Just before turning totally, he revolved back to her one more time, *Columbo*-like.

"Just remember what you're here for, Leyton, that's all. The door's unlocked by the way."

Leyton was almost moved by her boss's unexpected venture of tact as she strode up to the parked Volvo. A head could be made out in the back seat. *(Who on earth's this, he's sent me to deal with... as if a pair of murders isn't more important?)* She wondered, standing there a moment. Left with one way to find out, she grabbed the handle and opened instantly, to inspect his new client.

"Hello." came the lone passenger's voice that she, with horror, instantly recognised.

"Oh, my g..."

(iii)

As a serving detective, Leyton been used to all sorts of unexpected faces sitting in the back of their car in a pair of

120

handcuffs, but when that person in question happened to be Robbie Draycott, something definitely had to be wrong!

"Robbie, what's happened?"
"It was Mr Hargreaves! He arrested me! He made me get in the car!"
"For what? What can you have done wrong?"
"He said it's for being out running in a public place before eight o'clock a.m. He said I'm illegal. He said it's committing a crime."
"My g...." Leyton cut her last syllable, short of being actually sick.
"Sorry, Miss Jo. Sorry I'm a criminal."
"You're *not* a criminal, Robbie Draycott, don't ever think that of yourself! That title belongs to the man who brought you here in this car."

Leyton rummaged amongst a heap of clutter on Hargreaves's atrociously mal-organized dashboard. Being the negligent apology for a police officer, enough to leave them in his car, there should have been a set of keys for those cuffs. Scrabbling around under various sheets of paper and decaying documents, she heard something go to the floor with a faint metallic chink.

"Ah, here we go. Right, Robbie would you just like to lift your hands up?" she leant over with the key as he obliged, "Good lad...and you're a free man again."
"Can I go home now? I need to get to work."
"I ought to ring DC Garstone first - you remember him - and tell them we've found you. Can you just stay in the car a few minutes?"

She climbed back out, looking to see a place where she could assure herself of a bit of privacy amongst the parked vehicles for this call. It was to little avail with Hargreaves only five yards away, leant against Armitage's Focus while conversing with other scene officers.

(Oh bloody hell, where do I go to pull this one off?)

Leyton toured her sights a full 360 degrees, hoping for the solution to land... then it duly did. The 'Magic White Tent' was rising. *Brilliant,* she thought; if she could tiptoe right across the cycle course without Hargreaves having reasons for suspecting his newfound trust in her was misplaced, this would be the ideal safe haven.

"Leyton, you finished with 'face-ache' yet?" he clocked her unexpectedly. "It's nothing personal but you agreed on five minutes."
"It's okay sir, I'm done. Going straight back over as I talk, even."
"Seeing as the tent's nearer, why not help them with that? 'Mr Blobby' should be fine by himself. It's not as if he's alone, eh?"
"I suppose not." Leyton nodded in a reluctant agreement that was completely not so.

As he watched her go, Hargreaves returned to his own entourage. Coast clear, Leyton sprung across the tracks and into the tent. Her ruse had succeeded. Sounding more eager to assist with the body had got her placed with matters involving her favourite - the 'magic white tent' - instead and she knew that Hargreaves loved giving her the jobs she liked the least.

"Ma 'am ..."
"Excuse me, not now,"

She dismissed a forensic's intervention, elbowing her way through the miniscule marquee. Secreting herself out the back as much as possible, she began thrusting away at her mobile.

"Greg, unless you are at the wheel..."

"I could always take my hands off it."

"Only Hargreaves would ask you to risk your life that way." Leyton put her own volume low for more than one obvious reason "Listen. I've found Robbie, safe, so you can end the search and come straight over."

"Aye, nice one. Be three minutes, tops."

"Oh before you do, would you also do a quick favour: find out from HQ if Robbie's been made the unlikely subject of a fabricated arrest warrant?"

"Robbie? Why the hell would there be a writ on him?"

"Related to *who,* we believe, swiped Robbie from outside his doorstep this morning."

"Go on. Danny?   A mate of hi... my god, you saying it's ... *him*?" Garstone shook his head, hoping he didn't have to believe it. "I know the guy rides a shaky line between right and wrong, but, staging a phoney nick on a disabled kid? *BASTARD!*"

"Please try and get it confirmed, if possible - it's time I turned a few tables."

She heard no further response from Garstone right away but by the silence, it was as good as apparent to him who she entailed. The same, whose booming voice suddenly shattered the air... and her ears as well.

"L-E-E-EY-Y-Y-TO-O-O-O-N!!"

Clenching her eyes, she could only guess one reason why Hargreaves's voice had backslid into its brutish tones. Thrusting her mobile as far inside her jacket as it could hide, out of view (and her boss's suspicions of recent usage) she stepped one pace at a time from round the tent, both eyes almost shut.

7

INJUSTICE AND COURAGE

(i)

Leyton had a clear 50-50 bet over the first line from Hargreaves, being either "You breathed a single word down that phone..." or "How long does it take to stick a couple of bloody tent pegs in?" and was naturally praying it would turn out the latter.

(Here goes) She opened her eyes fully but kept a mental seatbelt fastened, even though aware the Superintendent had lightened his tone since the morning. A shame it was all to end with a single shuddering crash.

Hargreaves's vehicle, the only one on the field not sporting police paintwork was where Robbie still sat, inevitably fearing for his fate and also close to where its dastardly owner hovered alongside his other constabulary chums. For Leyton, it was best to coast coolly over to the body and appear busy.

"Right, what's the story so far," she blindly fired her first words in Armitage's direction, "apart from 'collided with a deranged individual's Stanley kni...'"
"Leyton!"

That voice again - he hit right on time, drowning out any response Armitage could summon. Her endeavours to elude Hargreaves proven as futile as ever, she rotated to notice her DCS walking right out from the tent as if he'd been hiding there all along. There was an unusually subdued expression sitting on Hargreaves face as he approached.

"I'm off up to the top end now so if you've got room in the back for Herr Fruitcake, do as you will with him."

Leading her to the Volvo, he opened the door and tipped Robbie out. The boy had sat there all morning, gazing out through the window like a bored child in a china shop.

"Okay son, time for the outside world again... hey that's funny..." He noticed on Robbie's handcuffs had developed powers to undo themselves.
"Funny?!" Leyton put some selective words into his mouth. "As in: funny that he was picked up from outside his house by a person matching your very description?"
"I thought his being here would keep him out of mischief."

The Superintendent didn't delay to invent any justifications for his contemptible actions but his DI   read it all over his face, all too clear of his nature. Leyton actually had it in her, this time to point her finger straight in a superior's eye. It became literal, her prevarications stretched beyond their limit.

"The situation is clear as it gets," she gave it to him, glossy-eyed and furious, "What you have done is technically kidnapping - not withstanding the fact that he isn't on record as an offender!"
"Well, he's made up for it now - attempted escape from police custody."
"If you mean the handcuffs; that'll be me."

Hargreaves frothed at her like an over-boiling saucepan, the face round his eyes bypassing red right through to a terminally enraged purple.

"Yes that's right, sir - I sprung him." Still room to rub it in more, Leyton tried to make sure one or two others were listening. "So, that finds me guilty of…assisting an escape from police custody, right?"

Her DCS didn't answer immediately. He opened the door wide, dragging Robbie out onto the grass before returning at her with a threatening finger.

"Well congratulations, DI Leyton, you've just made the most suicidal career move of your entire life." Hargreaves contorted his eyes into a patronising grimace. "I'll see you back at the station. Bring a handbag to clear your desk into - along with something just a marginal tad bigger … to throw yourself in as well."

With that he hulked away, slamming the Volvo's door shut as he left. Making little attempt to swallow these words for she knew she bore the moral high ground, Leyton had also seen rid of the man at an ideal moment. On top of this she was hoping that his return to the Harvester's Plough scene, *or* complete disappearance from Totley altogether would allow Garstone time to do his part.

"What's happening wi' this chap then?" Armitage asked, helping Robbie up.
"Well Mr 'caring', there seemed unprepared to grudge him a lift."
"Hey, why don't I take him- it's not as if he lives 500 miles away is it?" he invited Robbie towards the Focus "Come on kiddo, I'll run you back."
"Are you sure you should, Leroy?"

Leyton failed to welcome the idea, the 'second scar' topic dogging her once more as she noted it, still there in all its hideousness.

"" I don't want you scaring her as well."

"It's ok, Jo," Robbie backed him. "She's met him before, do you remember? She knows who he is, she does."

"Yes, that's what worries me."

Leyton shrugged and accepted, remembering. After all, allowing this would finally secure her space to investigate the latest poor devil unlucky enough to encounter the 'Totley Throttler', the only significant downside being she was now stranded, minus either her two star players.

"Weren't Greg meant to be back, now we're in the clear over El Robbo's whereabouts?" Armitage asked, conclusively.

"He's just trying to get *in the clear* a little further." Leyton winked. "Okay then, take 'trouble' home and be quick. No stopping round for a 'cuppa', remember." She looked fondly at her other friend. "Bye Robbie."

"See you soon." Robbie reverted to a cheerier tone now alongside his other favourite officer. "Take care yourself."

Leyton watched Armitage escort him warmly to the Focus like a dad picking his kids up after school, then prepared for another trek down the mushy green/brown matter towards her principal duties. On her way, she couldn't help but glimpse an irregularity in one of the tyre marks. Like a badly laid railway these particular ones seemed to travel downhill, any way apart from straight, graduating into a waving snake. It dissolved off into the sandstone path though a distinct termination in the prints could still be found.

(Not even a ruffian such as DCS Hargreaves could match such poor coordination… unless Robbie had perhaps distracted him en route.)

She felt the old fabled finger trick coming up inside. Closing her eyes Leyton created a vision of it, wiggling along the tyre line that disappeared to nowhere and then back out, tracing the direction in reverse.

Up to the gate... and back down again to the bike track... now back up again... the trajectory was developing. It appeared clearer - this giant melted layer of mint-chocolate ice cream that she stood on yielded visions of the last journey taken by the killer. An image that recruited a new object, passing also from the tracks up to the gate and down again.

A new object resembling a woman's arm, clad in a grey jacket sleeve swayed ahead like a pendulum; one that Leyton could feel tugging the rest of her body, softly then suddenly quite harshly. A second arm, a man's clad in high-visibility yellow appeared from nowhere to clamp round her elbow.

"D.I. Leyton. Are you alright?" a shrill voice followed.

Reintroduced to her senses, she turned to find it had been PC Raylesthorpe tugging her.

"Er...yes thanks." she responded though not sure who to.

Seeing nearly everyone, except about three of the investigative personnel had become mere spectators Leyton yanked herself hastily back to the here-and-now before her withdrawal became a visible worry to the others. Hijacked as she was by her dwindling psychological health, she had to carry on her investigation at some point, and pressed on after another second or so of troubled thinking.

Finding the cordon tape so low that ducking under would mean her knees in the mud, she let Raylesthorpe lift it, but the manners did not flatter her any more. Without coming across as personal -

it appeared she could barely care less. Aside from the victims being male the latest 'slash-n'-shoot', as often known in her previous department's parlance, brought practically nothing new to the table otherwise.

Leyton looked from back in the day when a trek across suburban Wrangleford wasteland normally ended looking into the corpse of some unfortunate doe-eyed beauty who'd paid highly for a dangerous taste in men. All tyre marks and no hall marks, this latest bump-off offered nothing exceptional enough to turn her aside from the Hargreaves/Robbie developments. Her current mortal could himself be just someone who'd suffered from an erratic choice of friends. 'Snap' again with the over-vegetated state of the long unused stunt course, deteriorated enough to earn the 'wasteland' tag itself.

Leyton no longer thought she was seeing anything special, drifting through the details by this stage as overblown circumstantial evidence exaggerated for her preferences - a psychological garden roller that flattened the sharpest aspects of this case right into the grass.

"*S-o-o,* now I've finally joined you, what else have you had found time to discover?"

Leyton made her demands just loud enough to be heard by all the gathered officers overseeing the examination.

"Well..." began Raylesthorpe in barely mangled words, "Nothing's shown up just yet - nothing of relevance to the crime, that is." He obviously wasn't about to tell D.I. Leyton that a Stanley knife had descended magically out of the clouds.
"This poor chap's body itself must have dropped out of *somewhere* to land here..." Leyton sounded like she'd actually heard him aloud "probably from a car door,"

"I beg your pardon for arguing, ma'am, but this might not be the case."

"Ok... Tell me I'm stupid, as usual. What have I not seen this time?"

Raylesthorpe showed her the tracks down from the gate, without admitting he'd just seen her looking right at them. To Leyton, they certainly didn't resemble anything a police car might have left behind.

"I see them. So what else am I missing?"

"I'm only hinting the driver must've possessed a superhuman throw to chuck this gent - whatever his name is - all that way."

"Donaldson." broke in one of the other officers," Nigel Donaldson, ma'am. Looks like they weren't after his money. His wallet was loaded, though a bit soggy from the puddle."

He pointed casually at the splash pool near the body, buried underneath rancid blackening leaves as well as mud from countless BMX tyres bygone.

"Okay boys," She foghorned at the entire team, making the pathology contingent shed their concentration "Can we have some shots of the tyres please? All angles."

"What about his wallet, ma'am?" asked Raylesthorpe.

"It doesn't directly relate at this stage, though I am still wondering how it would land straight into that whatever-you-want-to-call-it there,"

(*As if throwing a corpse from a car would send his wallet flying five yards, to so-coincidentally touch down on that exact spot*)

"*If* he was thrown, ma'am. The footprints suffered a bit from the rain, but are still discernible."

"Oh, of course, sorry."

"You *are* ok, aren't you, Detective Inspector?"

Little use in suppressing the fact that she wasn't, Leyton had walked into the scene and instantly been filled in yet she now had to ask everything about the crime, all over again. Her attitude had become steadily standoffish this morning, as if she was viewing the scene in her sleep. Hardly looking anyone straight in the eye Leyton watched the top of the field, every single visitor and vehicle alike, coming or going now mystifying her.

"I'm fine... I think," Leyton tried to fob off Raylesthorpe's concerns.
"Just couldn't help noticing you seemed upset by that earlier business with the Super. We can handle this scene ourselves ma'am, if you'd rather be going."
"I'm only here because Greg, and now also Leroy, *aren't!*" Leyton now snapped, resenting Raylesthorpe's constant inquests as much as she did Armitage's. "So if we just get back to matters in hand, do you mind presenting me with these footprints you've been rambling on about?"

Obliging without delay, in case she was about to lose her cool with him as well, Raylesthorpe pointed out a small series of craters in the grass, still unsure as how she would take it with her turn in mood.

"Sorry they're not very good - as I said already. We haven't yet confirmed they are footprints. Could be plant pots even, or..."
"Its alright, Mike, I'm perfectly sure a human foot's guilty, one with a nice cushy shoe to hide inside."

By the irregularity of the route, it did appear Mr Donaldson could have possibly been coming to land from this mythical mid-air flight that Raylesthorpe believed in.

"Forgive me if I sound a bit cocky here, ma'am but when someone has it on his toes from a bloke with a knife, won't his strides be a whole lot bigger?"

"So you're saying he *didn't* get thrown, now, are you?" Leyton became even more churned by his burbling lines.

"No, I was just saying..."

"Save it, I've had enough confusion for one day!"

He paused to try re-phrasing his opinion but it was too late, the words already out were what Leyton registered. She snatched out the tyre mark photo, nearly dragging the camera off the pathologist's head. Leyton needed to go elsewhere to think things over, unhindered seeing that her fuse was, as the officers could clearly see at this stage singed a little short.

"Ma'am, we've only got one photo of the tyre prints so far - the one you're holding."

"Well bloody well take another one!" She used the voice of someone talking to a five year old, thinly disguising that of someone who was basically grumpy. "Or better still, deal with the shoe prints instead! You could have done that by now instead of just talking!"

Ending on those words, she stumped off back towards the Magic White Tent, shielding the photo under her lapel in distrust of the weather.

(ii)

Past caring any more what they were thinking, and at the same time fighting to ignore the Hargreaves/Robbie fiasco for the while, Leyton ensconced herself in the now vacated tent. Placing her cool just short of throwing the plastic red chair across the other side, she banged the photo flat on the table and tiredly dragged out her biro, marking rings round the tracks.

She forced her currently mis-aligned concentration on the vision she was hoping to filter out of the small 4" by 3" print. Creating a scale reconstruction using half her purse's contents to double for objects, she placed the gate (*Koffee Kingdom* loyalty card) at the left of the table and then parked police vehicles (a selection of used rail tickets) filing out the far side.

(Hold on, police vehic…)

She realized something was a little premature for the actual time of the incident, moving the tickets back away to plant a hedge instead. It took fifteen long seconds of fingernails between teeth before she made the initial moves with the killer's car (top-up card from her spare mobile). Lifting the gate aside instead of crashing it down as the offender had, she pushed the car in, batting it slowly across the field (table) with her fingernails before finally slewing it into a right angle over the photo, which now doubled as the stunt area.

She thought again… (*That makes sense so far. The oh-so-bloody-typical entry of a serial murderer in his motor, no question about that!*) Leyton suddenly appreciated the clearer picture. *Now for that 'superhuman' throw Raylesthorpe was on about. This person is someone of anything up to seven feet in height AND with, possibly, the strength to lift a phone booth).*

Her train of thought ended the tyre prints right below where Raylesthorpe's had taken the shot.

Okey dokey, then…his stature is as I guessed - he's got legs long enough for strides so big with several tons of body over his shoulder. I think I'm beginning to like this now.

Music suddenly came to her ears, literally as the vibration hit home. Strange, it though seemed that the chorus from her favourite '*Coldplay*' number should be automatically performed to command her alertness. A couple of seconds was taken recognising her Ericsson's ringtone as the generous provider.

"You coming back up here today?" Garstone confirmed the disturbance as his doing.
"Well probably, now you've finally reached *there*, i.e. the Harvester's Plough, yourself." Leyton replied smartly, pausing to adjust the audible lack of gratitude in her voice. "So, any treasures since I set sail away to the 'other' islands?"
"Yeah, we've unearthed his identity at last, and all without disturbing the body."
"Great. So-o-o what did our third unlucky victim go by the name of?"

Garstone went silent for a few seconds as if he'd suddenly switched off, too.

"*Somebody...Donaldson*, it says," he broke off while trying to read "... can't quite get to his surname, something's got stuck on it...think it's '*Pete*' though."

Leyton nearly knocked the table, with all her props to the floor, the instant the name came into the air.

"Could you just run that surname by me again?" she asked, if just to establish that her hearing wasn't vanishing in the same direction as her marbles this afternoon "Donald..."
"Son...yeah, that's right. You're gonna ask me next if he's got a duck for a dad?"
"Well I noticed they look alike, well *did* until..."
"Until..."

He waited for the rest but it didn't seem ready to come. The newly intellectually- challenged DI appeared to have lost it again, disguising this very thinly to her partner.

"Unt…. oh forget it," she finally gave in to the strain "Nothing important anyway. Seen Hargreaves?"

"The guv just shot by as I turned up. Only had time for a couple of things - one being the guy you got down there wound up on the wrong end of a Stanley blade…."

" And the second one involving the words 'Get *your arse down there?*'"

"Actually more like '*Have been summoned immediately back to Midelson Rd HQ*'"

"So the drinks are on you tonight then, are they?"

"No, tonight they're on Bill, the landlord."

"Oh, Greg, why did you have to get him involved?"

"Appears you're his new best mate, if I believe what you've done is right. He wasn't too chuffed at seeing our beloved DCS outside the pub door."

"We all know that feeling,"

Leyton 's nonchalant reaction wasn't too much of a problem for Garstone as he had a tale lined up to tell for once, today: he wasn't about to delay with it either.

"Leroy's just had to restrain Bill from setting his dogs on the bloke."

"What the hell's Leroy playing at - he's supposed to be taking Robbie home. Not to mention the fact that Hargreaves's favourite prisoner was also sat in the front."

"Its ok, he ducked." Garstone whipped the usual most pathetic excuse out of the hat -a quiet reaction from her reading as 'passed.' "Anyway, what's the story with these footprints?"

"Footprints?" Leyton sounded lost once more "I only remember finding tracks leading down from the pub, but nothing trainer-shaped."

"Looks like there were two of them then. One running, one driving. Both guys stuck their rubber in the same mud, there's no mistake there. I didn't spot the tracks at first, myself - they suddenly appeared, like magic."
"He seems to have a very athletic accomplice."

Leyton commended, picturing the maniacal rate at which the car would have shot down Totley Hall Lane then returned doubly fast heading out. An average getaway speed along this type of road would be in the region of 30mph. That was above twice what most able-bodied humans would run at.

"Well, there you go then," Garstone tried to quell the unnecessary to-do she'd made of the point. "What you worryin' about? Told you I thought there was more than one."

Leyton was however not prepared to be made to feel stupid this time for she was more in the picture, albeit in a different frame.

"This does not add up, Greg. More like '*down*' in fact. There are only four footprints, and even all of these located within a tight vicinity of the body itsel..."
"MA'AM!"

A shout came from one of the analysts, making her nearly drop the mobile into the wet vegetation. Leyton tottered over as one of the officers extended his arm swinging an object precariously between his white-gloved fingers. Her eyes shot wide, as if lodged with invisible matchsticks, spotting what they'd just plucked out of the grassy depths.

Garstone and the also-returned Armitage witnessed a grin on Leyton's face appear as she strode up the drive of the Harvester's Plough - the reason for this they had to hear right away.

"I see why you couldn't get all the way down again." She dodged round the cordon that cut off the complete road to all but uniformed cars.

"*S-o-o* what have you got then?" Garstone confidently selected his first few words to welcome her back "You look right happy all of a sudden."

"Looks like its two-nil to '*Leyton*' Orient now."

Leyton produced the bag in front of his face waving it slowly enough for him to see a yellow-bodied instrument bearing the word Proto-Cut in faded green down the side.

"What you on about… *two nil?*"

"I said, didn't I - Mr Donaldson was killed right there on the stunt course…"

"Said you couldn't rule it out. One-nil-plus-near-miss-penalty, I'd make it. Still susses things a bit, that way. What about his brother though?"

"Er…. are you sure about that?"

Leyton asked this, not knowing at all why for, but her reactions were becoming increasingly glib and indirect by the minute. Armitage seemed just as befuddled by this question from such an intelligent woman; it was like he and Garstone were turning to cardboard figures right there in front of her.

"How come you're asking us that?" he dared to comment "You're the one whose been there all day, ma'am, should be the other way."

"No silly, about the 'brother' thing. You're great jokers, lads but the day I fall for that one again,"

"This'll wipe the laugh off your face, miss smarty-socks."

Garstone handed her a rag of stiffened card extracted from the wallet near Peter Donaldson's body. Leyton unfolded it to see a pair of photo cabin pictures, taken clearly not long before his murder.

"Two-all then, I take it." She accepted defeat for the first time today.
"Y'think he…whatever his bro's name is, were also in the garden when it happened?"
"His brother's name is Nigel," she sternly adjusted his sentence, "and yes, I am pretty sure he was. The prints do say it all now."
"Say what?"
"How would you like me to start, *doctor*?"

Leyton began blathering, in her normal convoluted delivery, cue Armitage's settling on a nearby bollard but halfway in she was wasting her breath - they saw now the process of Nigel's Donaldson's demise like clear-cut glass. Arriving in the garden to see his brother being attacked, this still unidentified party immediately became aware of his presence, dropping Peter to confront him instead.

Ye-e-e-e-s she eased it in to her conscience.

Scarcely dodging an initial attack right there, the surviving sibling fled before the killer could manage a proper lunge. Seemingly of good physique himself, 'Nigel' had ran the entire half-mile of Totley Hall Lane in only three minutes, and eventually broken loose… so he'd thought. The killer's getaway driver, who'd obviously got his job description confused followed down in the car mere seconds later and parked up whilst watching his friend pile in with the blade.

(Alternatively the victim was pulled to the ground and forced to lose the wallet, before being slaughtered in the resultant struggle, trying to pull himself to safety. The culprit already carried the Stanley in his hand, from cutting his calling-sign into

the wood so it was a piss-easy murder from his viewpoint)

All three dwelled on both these possibilities, circling butterfly-like amidst their minds, as they looked at each other, yet this one last conundrum hung.

"Hmm, so few footsteps for two people's involvement." Leyton rocked the boat again.
"Where did you say the blade were found?" Armitage asked.
"Bottom of a hedge, apparently. Well to be truthful, Mike said that, not me."
"You've got the footprints coming back up the road again?"
"No, these are the prints from the *field*, you sodding lemon! *They're* what I'm on about; those four mysterious holes in the grass, remember them?"

Leyton shook her head, terminally exasperated by them both, and stormed away inside the pub.

"Thanks mate." said Garstone hinting that Armitage had opened his trap at the handiest of times once again.

(iii)

Getting a piping hot pub coffee down Joanne Leyton's neck seemed the one curative avenue for her crippled self-confidence, at least by Garstone's belief. As both DCs chatted away with Bill Rawlinson, the Harvester's friendly landlord, he couldn't help but become distracted by the sight of his boss. With a face like a lifelong gambler after losing their first ever bet, Leyton sat slumped, head underneath one hand at a window-side table, reluctantly slurping her somewhat over-milked brew.

Garstone remembered having nearly won her back earlier outside with their latest 'scoop' of sorts, only for Armitage's ill-timed attempt at an innocent joke to see it all come undone. Thus with the team's effort to pluck her from the doldrums doomed again to fail, some useful information from the Harvester's Plough faculty may just heighten spirits. It would of course help if Garstone paid attention to the discussion they were currently engaged in. Despite his erudite nature, Bill's joviality, for a man who'd just had to put up with a murder in his garden knocked the detectives for six. His small lips, almost camouflaged amidst the rest of his stubbly square face stayed in a smile-like shape, making his emotions hard to distinguish. Garstone wouldn't have helped but begun to suspect the chap, were it not for himself also disconnecting a bit.

"Wakey, wakey, mate," Armitage retrieved him. "Don't you go off into cloud country on me too."
"I'm not, Lee but I'm wondering if we did the right thing, telling her just like that."
"I thought that were my fault."
"Nah, it was just random talk I launched into for the hell of it really. I try too hard, more than you do sometimes."
"She your boss then, is she?" said Bill, also noticing.
"Aye, afraid so." said Armitage.
"Hey, watch it..." Garstone warned, "She's still your DI, whatever state she's in,"

He became momentarily stern again; startling Armitage who realised some weren't that much in the mood for fun and games yet.

"Now, back to the task in hand, if you don't mind," Garstone firmly urged him to continue. "and I don't just mean our beloved DI."
"For a minute, I though it were your mate Hargreaves you was on

140

about then." chuckled Bill, "Using the word 'mate' loosely there."

"Ah," Garstone saw reason to lighten once again,"You saying you've got a history with our possibly-soon to be *ex*-DCS?"

"Aye, as Mr Armitage there will tell you."

As Bill revolved on his barrel-like frame to run Garstone's coffee, the two detectives looked at one another, both competing to becoming the most sidetracked by the irregularities taking shape.

"Walked in, slung one at our lass Stella, we slung him out again. Nothing much left to tell."

This was as always a total lie from Bill who before long was inflicting the ins and outs on them in good old inn-keeper parlance. (*In short, Hargreaves, somewhat the worse for seven post-duty pints, had thrown a drip tray across the counter at Bill's barmaid daughter after being refused further service.*)

As the tale, laid out in never ending pieces, started to go over the top of Garstone's head, it had already cruised straight over Leyton's. By now left totally out of the conversation, she drifted yet further from the real world while the male-only committee behind continued inaudibly. Her boss's name seemed to flutter by amidst chequers of insignificant words she occasionally caught. By the time Bill reached the part about successfully turning the tables on Hargreaves with the Pubwatch policy, she heard everything around her grow faint, right down to the almost dead-altogether. Hunched ever more forward in her chair, she was reduced to merely visioning figures and faces passing her, in the pub, around her and elsewhere.

One was right there in her head. Hargreaves. (*So that man had, not for the first time crossed the line.*) As her reflection showed

141

in her coffee, it swirled round with the liquid, clearly functioning in synchrony with her mind. A second face welled into sight next to it... one with an unmistakable moustache.

Friday, October the 28th had suddenly evolved into a day of reckoning for Leyton.   She had plenty there to back her actions up but was it enough to get her out of her tunnel? Hargreaves had been well and truly caught with his pants down, tonight, but were the words of two Detective Constables enough weight to crush him?

(Possibly not. Only Leroy has been there long enough to witness 'Hargreaves Horrendous Misadventures' at their previous worst. Clearly the danger was that if he'd kept his job following that last pub episode, what else could he brush under the carpet?)

Hargreaves already knew Robbie had got off, scot-free over the fairground incident - was that what inclined him to retribution?

(Rubbish!   It was nothing at all to do with Robbie, basically just Hargreaves's cheap excuse to persecute a vulnerable timid individual without any form of legal sanction. He'd acquired Robbie's address either on the grapevine, or a certain Detective constable's carelessness and just lie waiting outside for him.)

In short Hargreaves was either punishing Robbie the way his hatred for people of non-conforming creed compelled him, or Leyton for releasing him.

(So Robbie and I are just as bad as one another, ARE WE? He's a common crook because he has a nervous breakdown in public, IS HE? Meanwhile I'm a bad cop because I release him without charge, WITHOUT my Superintendent having chance to get his oar in, AM I? It that it?)

It turned Leyton bitter dealing with it - drawing parallels with the days when her father was caned for left-handedness. She was forced to feel again what John Leyton himself went through, of Mr Pellingstone punishing him, like a criminal, for a natural human trait - *that* old bastard and Hargreaves seemed to weld into one here. As she let this memory drag her down slowly with the rest of her depressions, she rubbed her index finger along her lip in agitation.

Her own prison-comparable school life began to blend in with it; every morning finding her way barred by the fearsome fluorescent-socked figure of Amy Collinson - fifth form's top girl - outside the bike shed.

"Oi, what did I warn you yesterday about Beatles shirts in this yard?"

Along with fellow tomboys Veronica Templeton and Tracy Granger, the savage kangaroo court ambushed its favourite client daily, her two henchwomen forming the bench and jury.

"Joanne Leyton, we find you guilty of constant infringement of the Taste and Image act, 1987."

Punishment normally came swift - lenient being pushed to the ground and having her blouse ripped open, then her hair ruffled up into a 'Bananarama' style perm.

"Dissenter, Dissenter." The other two chanted as Leyton was subject to the same daily ordeal.

This carousel in her head began spinning faster, powered by the heckle. The horses beginning to break from it, *'Mary Poppins'-like,* circled her... all sporting the faces of her enemies past and present.

(DISSENTER! DISSENTER!) You disrespect our laws (DISSENTER! DISSENTER!) You do not conform... (DISSENTERS! DISSENTERS!) You...Robbie...your dad... (DISSENTERS! DISSENTERS!) You deserve to burn.... You deserve to pay.... (DISSENTERS, DISSENTERS DIE!)

Leyton felt excessively pressured towards letting it out before her real life audience, but at the same time a countermanding notion, aggravated by the risk of appearing even crazier, rammed her head from the other direction.

Biting down on her finger in frustration, the two-way mental torture persisted: two plates of the earth's crust pressing together either side of her dangerously volcano-like mind, driven from opposite ends by this harrowing multitude of troubles. She bit further, fighting the pressure she now endured by a thread.

She drooped further, her forehead almost meeting the table. A hot glare rose into her eyes but all still visible, was her inner torments spinning inside. Ignoring this extra heat, Leyton battled all that now pounded inwards preparing to crush her but something hotter, much more unbearable, came through it: boiling ...like a liquid, possibly lava between the two 'plates', rising.

It stung her and violently so, as if her face was set alight. Receding from the other self-imagined fires of hell she'd roasted in, this last half an hour, a massive knock to the back of her hair made her almost topple off her seat.

"JO!"

A frantic voice resonated loudly from close. She just caught the shape of a tall male making across towards her.

144

Leyton had spent an hour trying to convince both Armitage and Garstone that she was fully back on track with reality: it was working but in shaky stages. Supplying her with drinks and hot food on the house, to help her that last step of the way home Bill was also wallowing in their concern, as well as repaying a certain favour from earlier.

"Just as I though you'd got over it," Garstone said as he staggered over with another coffee, replacing one that Leyton had more or less sent to the floor. "It appears we just didn't try hard enough. Yet on our third attempt... we may-y-y have succeeded."

(*It did seem like a prolonged panic attack.*) Leyton tried to build up her answer without recapturing the right words, though the bang she'd took on the head looked to have finally done its trick. Figuring that this was what had revived her, Leyton only wished she'd fallen into that coffee thirty minutes sooner than she did.

"So, when you're ready to begin," Garstone set about his own interrogation "what happened?"

Before Leyton even spoke it was observably worse than what had switched on her waterworks last night. The above-disturbing emotional outbreak Garstone had just witnessed signals of an issue still plaguing her, she felt was too painful to reveal. Her ever persistent DC was hell-bent on driving it out of her but how could she guaranteed it would be heard without just laddish ridicule? Garstone had caught wind of her earlier flare-ups towards Raylesthorpe and the forensics team - perhaps that's what she was now answering for.

"I don't know really." she started away with the usual one "I've been sat on my own for ages. The consequences of what I've done to Derek are getting to me, I admit."

"So you *were* still with us then? God don't tell us all this has been you acting."

"I listened for a while - only remember something about Hargreaves laying into a barmaid some while ago."

"If you remembered that much, you surely didn't suffer a total space-out, so congratulations."

"I must say though, Greg I surely don't remember ordering food from the bar."

She found herself staring down at a large Yorkshire pudding filled with sausages and onions. Leyton curiously surveyed the plate of food seemingly given to her either on the pub, or two guiltily generous police officers, but didn't yet move to consume it. Garstone pushed it a little further towards her so she could savour the aroma of gravy.

"What is this supposed to be anyway?"

"It's called a 'Yorkshireman', that," said Armitage. "Bill's thanks for what you did with the Super'. Don't matter if you're not hungry, we'll take care of i…"

"*A-a-a!*" "Bill invaded, shooing both of them aside "You two each have your own platefuls, sat there going cold."

"Oh, you haven't…!"

Leyton rose halfway up, just enough to spot the massive platefuls of scrumptious pub food on their places by the bar as well - exactly the same dish as hers, and also little touched.

"He certainly has." Garstone slipped the disturbing fact that Bill had treated Armitage as well.

"Well Leroy should have no problem murdering that, not that I'd want to observe his party trick with the leftover gravy."

146

"Is this you pretending that you're the full way back from cuckoo land, or have you actually made it this time?"

"Once I eventually manage to taste this so-called 'food', Greg, I'll have a better idea."

Garstone could tell that Leyton's turn-back was far from realistic yet he tried his hardest yet to siphon truthful words out of her. She knew he intended watching her till she tried the food, so knowing it was the only way out, took up her fork, attacking one of the sausage pieces with a melodramatic nibble.

Each mouthful a step towards her recovery, he casually monitored Leyton's slow destruction of the Yorkshireman, glad at least that she was eating it, full stop. Bill had cooked that meal on the understanding it would help her, having been pretty distraught to find this impeccably courageous officer reduced to a neurotic mess at his first meet with her in person.

"That's not bad." Leyton suddenly declared.

"Not bad? Is that all Bill's cooking gets, heh?"

"Think she'd enjoy it better with this," Bill brought her latest steaming mug of Starbucks across.

"I think Leroy's just 'suffering the consequences' as we speak."

Garstone noticed Armitage's chair was vacant. *(Christ on a bike; give the man free food and you give him a licence to waste it.)* He eyed the other plate of sausage, onion and *surviving* Yorkshire pud on the table. *('kay, well, if HE ain't gonna be touching it again)* An explosion of laughs stopped him dead in his tracks as his friend re-appeared from the door, holding his mobile.

"Fancy sharing the joke?"

"Aye. Ma'am, get this." Armitage walked straight over to Leyton. "PC Raymond's just been on from t'station - guess what!

147

Super's got him'sen suspended!"

"Yes-s-s." Leyton clenched her fist victoriously, smiling fully at last.

She didn't have a heavy enough heart to poop the party by telling them that Hargreaves's predicament had only reached to an initial hearing at this time. The Superintendent was obviously discharged with immediate effect pending the outcome of her allegations; that went without saying but still, she had to big this up to them as grandly as possible.

"That's gonna cheer a few guys up at the station." Garstone wallowed openly "A new era of crime investigations without prejudice, coming right up, eh?"
"Only for now. Our Complaints Authority chummies still need to talk to Robbie and his family before Hargreaves gets dunked the full way underwater."

Leyton weighed up - finding hard to accept here that procedure applied irrespective of how much their DCS deserved everything that might be coming to him. She caught Garstone facing in another direction, obviously not listening.

"It's ok." he said, "Was just wondering what Bill's laughing at… my god!!!"

Garstone stormed across, practically frogmarching Armitage with him. His face reddened, having seen Bill was in fits studying a gallery of photos from the previous year's Halloween evening. One of the snaps portrayed a tall short-skirted witch with ill-fitting green-black striped tights clutching a luminous yellow wand, the face of Garstone under the hat just clear enough to recognise.

"Forgot all about that, mate, honest." shivered Armitage.

"Unlucky for you I remember then. Now, lower it before *she* ....oh god, too late."

"Too late for what?"   Leyton demanded, joining."

Armitage tried to block the picture, but once seeing Garstone's near- convincing effort at fancy dress she lapsed into another seizure, albeit of laughter. Armitage bailed him out with the fact that Garstone was new by a week at Midelson Road department when he donned the outfit, the 2010 function doubling as his 'initiation'.

Garstone seemed heavily unconcerned with embarrassment, now satisfied he had his DI back again. He managed to squeeze out some choice words in reference to Armitage's own outfit for that memorable night, at which both saw their turn to crease up.

"Too late to find Batman the right coloured tights, I'd say."

"So what's it going t'be tomorrow then?"   Bill composed himself, pointing to the large orange poster alongside.

'Harv-o-Ween Horror Fest, Saturday October 29th. Hauntingly Huge Prizes for Best Dressed'.

"Well Hargreaves came as Widow Twankey last year." Garstone recollected.

"Oh, so his previous attempt at getting barred for life failed did it?"

"As if he ain't been doing enough dressing up in his life already," Armitage added further water to the boil," The bloke's been turning up at work each year, the last thirty years, pretending he's a copper."

All four were defeated by humour - the first time in their entire working history both Garstone and Leyton had found one of Armitage's jokes funny. Leyton had struggled to smile for nine

149

hours, eat for the last twelve and now here she was closely avoiding indigestion, splitting her sides at one of the most profound insults set aside for her DCS, yet.

"Hello....." Armitage tried to collect an untimely radio interruption *"Aye, she is....* Ma'am, Will wants a word."
"Will he? "

Leyton struggled to come down to earth from the other direction containing her newfound light-heartedness as serious business set foot once more.

"Hello-o...?"
"Are *you* free, ma'am? I'm near the top of Butts Hill along with PC Collins."
"Butt's Hill? Where on earth's that supposed to be?" She almost sniffed a further joke but disciplined herself.
"Across the road, almost literally - and could do with you coming right over."
"Go on then... "She picked her plate up, asking Bill "Can you either put this in the fridge, or let someone - or *some-two* - else take care of it between them?"
She rolled eyes, at them, grabbing her jacket. "I'm afraid I have to nip out, boys. You just behave with that food."
"Something we don't need to know about then?" Garstone asked.
"Will didn't mention either of you two, but stop around for a bit just in case."

Leyton stepped out of the top door and followed the blue just beyond the junction. Unlike she expected the PC was not stood waving to her this time.

"Will?" She called out, approaching where Thompson's unit was parked, at the Totley Church School gateway. "So what's so interesting here that you had me dragged from my dinner?"
"Over there."

Thompson pointed from the door while PC Collins rummaged in the boot for a light. Leyton could just make out a collection of recreational structures in the schoolyard. A swing and roundabout were partly visible in the shadow.

"Oh come on now, Will. Just because we're used to it a lot recently, it doesn't mean every children's swing we pass by's got someone strung from the top."

Leyton couldn't see anything so Thompson obviously had to elaborate his findings a little.

"I'd advise you to think more 'roundabout' than 'swing', ma'am." He then called back over to his friend "Tim, have you got the torch yet?"
"Nope, it's well hidden, mate." said the other young PC.

Without time to dawdle for it, Thompson turned the car headlights up. Looking from where Leyton was, the roundabout could be seen to be rotating extremely slowly. A flattish shape lay on the top, sprawled out and dark. Leyton stepped ahead towards it cautiously, ensuring she kept clear of the car light.

"I wouldn't't get too close ma'am. You did mention you'd just been eating."
" Ugh, God…"

Thompson was too late. She'd got three quarters of the way across, seeing it in full. Whatever was believed at first some random drunk, out for the count (with a risqué choice in bedding) turned to be even more asleep still, making her immediately regret ignoring the PC's advice. She cadged the radio from him, calling for Garstone.

"Boys, you've not got too much left on your plates - or *mine* - have you? You probably *will* be required across the road now."

8

LOST MINDS AND LOLLIPOPS

(i)

The grim object she saw, rotating vaguely right in front of her made Leyton glad of leaving that 'Yorkshireman' unfinished, although the fifth death in the last four days was hardly much more pleasant for PC Thompson either.

He'd only arrived six minutes before her, having heard the other vehicle driving recklessly away. It had clearly left in the Old Hay direction: no one was seen emerging onto the crossroads. Manning his unit with Collins to give chase, the sight of the school's gate left fully ajar swiped his attention.

Momentarily less concerned with the other car, whose registration they'd completely missed, Thompson backed up and turned halfway through the gate. Why would the roundabout in a private school playground be spinning at this time of night, he couldn't help but ponder.

Adjusting the headlight position slightly, he squinted his eyes at the scraggly shape laid across the bars. Thompson stepped out of his seat, edging round to approach whoever or whatever it might be, lying there.

"Christ...."

Feeling a bit guilty at uttering the Lord's name in vain right outside a Church of England property, one could barely restrain it on seeing a murder victim's body left like this.

153

This whole scene mirrored some ritual sacrifice aftermath. The man was spread-eagled across the roundabout, his face set straight at the sky. His arms and legs rested along the length of the holding bars as if fixed. The head fell back slightly as Thompson got right up, stopping the roundabout with his foot. As the eyes remained wide open, he felt some remaining breaths, but no lip movement accompanied. Although the face could not be told as pale, while discoloured by the headlamps something wet and glistening oozed snail trail-like from the side of his mouth.

"I'm surprised you managed to see even that detail, standing in your own lights," Leyton passively appraised Thompson's recital of the find. "Are you so tired that switching on a torch is too much labour for your fingers?"
"I couldn't find one in the car, so I thought it might..."
"Save the excuses till later, chatterbox. Let's just get the 'gang' back up... praying they're still about."
"What about the Magic White Tent? It's still down at the dirt track."
"We might need a magic *luminous* one this time." She sounded bright again as she pushed her way round Thompson. "Now, isn't it time I was introduced to our latest 'unlucky' devil?"

She mounted the roundabout to get a look at the liquid that Thompson had been rabbiting on about, tipping the man's head very carefully to the side. The slender dribble, a familiar red sort, which glinted with the saliva it mixed into, seemed to be coming from more than one place; it had already grown a considerable pool on the roundabout floor. Withdrawing her touch, she tried to check the other side of the head, blocking out her own light as well.

"We've got a fair old river of it here, ma'am," Thompson pointed

154

down at around where he stood, about three yards from Leyton. "I can't make out which part of him, from."

"We-ell..." Leyton drew a momentary conclusion, "it's from his mouth for one, but somewhere else round the body is a strong possibility for the *other*."
"I got the light, Will!" Collins called.
"I'd be careful Tim, the red's all around us!" he warned his friend bouncing across the yard, towards them.
"Blood?" Collins activated it at the floor in panic. "Can't see any in front of me."
"Try another five feet higher, but stay there - it's still moving."
"Yeah, got it here. Sticky end, he met judging by the spread of it."

The blood stopped halfway between him and Thompson. A near-rectangular spread, it looked to Leyton like the victim was dragged right from the car once more, with how the settled gore had spread.

"One second." She stopped him, crouched by the blood as Collins pointed "I can just make out a bit of floor at your end."

The red carpet hit a total end just short of Thompson's feet, cut over by a five-inch   interruption of chevron tread patterning. As Collins receded, a faint half-moon line appeared in the tarmac, like a 3D image, the floor disappearing into a vague background. The inner circle of the car marks came into show. Leyton let this fill her picture right to the point of convergence, though part of the route was covered over by Thompson's car.

"Seen it yet, ma'am?" Thompson badgered.
"I certainly have," judged Leyton.   "It looks like our friend fancied scoring a hat-trick today. He never even left Totley."

155

Barely half an hour later, the car park of Totley Church School was lit up like the city's Christmas lights although less colourful. However, everything and anything red, from Leyton's suit jacket to the stream of bloody mess stood out boldly in the applied whiteness. Whilst the hurriedly recalled forensics got to work, she had to shield her eyes whilst crossing between the glares of the portable floodlights. As if avoiding the now-browning blood trail was made difficult enough, the swarming bee's nest of officers hovering round the body, and each other, became similarly hazardous.

One welcome face, at least reappeared with the team tonight. Veteran pathologist Dr Donald Jamison, an old favourite of Leyton's had opted to step in, excusing Raylesthorpe and his party of 'work-experience'-standard analysts the agony.

The wispy, art-tutor-like beard which added another ten years onto his fifty-seven seemed to disappear beneath the glare, but his square-jawed head cut a penetrating shape above everyone (apart from when he crouched down).

The magnesium-like intensity of Jamison's light show brought an additional bonus for Leyton - people had nowhere to hide from her, pathologists and police officers alike becoming instantly spotlit, in through the gateway. A certain pair of trusty colleagues served up the most distinctive silhouette as they entered.

"Mind the lollipop," she warned Armitage as he stepped closer in, past Garstone.

As his cloth-eared misinterpretation diverted his mind to some sixties pop classic, Garstone took the hint quickly, pointing down on what he believed needed to be seen.

"Where the chuffin' pork-choppers is that from?" Armitage had to ask.

"It's most likely to be from the poor gent you see lying on top of that roundabout."

Leyton, accustomed to such gormlessness despite the strained escape from her own demons, showed him the trail while Garstone looked cautiously back to make sure his friend avoided stepping anywhere careless. As Armitage got by the sentries to join the 'roundabout' team, Garstone now held his stare to the blood.

"What's up, Greg? Are you not convinced I've recovered yet?"
"Aye, you sound like you're there - enough for our liking."

Leyton's faded seriousness seemed basically her slow adaptation to this freedom, with Hargreaves gone. Garstone appeared to be having his try at switching off now so she joined him to work out the distraction.

"It's just…." he pondered over, mystified by the mess "… just that the blood and the tyre tracks…."
"*They're the same set as over the road?* Yes indeed."
"I see where the 'lollipop' business comes in, no worries. (*Quick in- round -do whatever he did with the victim- and on his way again.)*"

He was puzzled alright, not by the truncation of the blood, where the tyres ran over but by something else that attracted his attention.

"Kinda fancy lookin', this ma'am."

Garstone directed his finger at the red nearest his side. New to Leyton also, the trail's edge didn't appear straight anymore, adopting a jagged ripple as if suddenly hit by static current.

157

"Don't know how best I could describe it off the top of my head."

Uninspired by his rambling, Leyton got down for a better glance. The thick river of crimson, now becoming a rusty tan, had widened during its wetter state but sustained a wavy line down just one side. Similar to the edge of a cloud, it continued with the edge, dipping at fourteen -inch intervals.

"Probably nothing, Greg." Leyton sounded not to read into it. (*Blood being a thicker substance than water, impact on level ground can have that effect on the spread.*)

"Looks like it's gonna be bigger than a casual slit round the throat this time."
"We haven't been able to locate it yet." said Thompson, "The DI and I found an exit trace from the mouth but it was unusually minimal, considering how it's filled the floor already. Only once we get the fellow lifted will we know any more."
"That's going to be rather difficult, I'm afraid." interrupted Jamison.

Beckoning Leyton back onto the roundabout, he lifted the man's right hand slightly. The steel glint, of what looked unmistakably like a handcuff showed in the light.

"Aye, nothing a certain little key can't fix," Garstone optimised aside the petty obstacle, unaware this situation wasn't a first for Leyton tonight.
"I hate to be the bearer of bad news again- well more like *awkward*." Jamison raised the left arm, pretending to struggle. "but I think you'll find more than just the standard manacles at hand here."

Leyton quickly saw why disengaging this latest body from his mountings wasn't exactly to be a two-second task. His legs, remaining arm plus waist were bound to the bars by separately cut portions of light industrial chain. Each end bayed by a heavy padlock, it appeared the guilty party had applied a bonus tourniquet.

"Leroy, what on earth are you doing?" She noticed Armitage sliding onto his back, underneath.
"Gonna 'ave a better look at them chains."
 "Just what use is that supposed to be, Albert Einstein? I'd have thought you might have noticed there are *padlocks*."
"There's got to be a bit of slack on them, someplace." Garstone neutralised this potential debate. "As long as Leroy's got the light we can get a better shufty at what we're cutting."
"It looks perfectly like chains and a padlock, to me," Leyton was lost again. "What cause have you possibly got for complication herein?"
"Well, that's what gets me thinkin' here." Garstone said, ushering her aside. "(*The guy makes this much a mess getting him out from the car, but takes the whole day   tying him up*) something kinda back to front here, right?"
"Only that the people we suspect involved might just have staged a role reversal of their previous escapade."
"What's to say there were two of them this time?"
"EH?!!!"

After all they'd discussed today, Leyton was shocked speechless to answer that from Garstone, he being the one who'd first insisted there were two in the team. She clung to her cool with difficulty as she explained that *firstly* engaging the victim to the roundabout was a task only realistically quick with two pairs of hands; *secondly* the murderer, with an adequate degree of logic would use his accomplice instead of adding more of his own prints into the carnage.

"I was coming in from that direction." Garstone vainly excused his own ignorance.

"Which direction?"

"The *not -two-of-them- but more-like-three* kind of direction."

"It's a possibility but that, only." Leyton appreciated that Garstone was halfway towards talking sense. "We're not going past '*more-than-one*' right now."

"So you still thinking the guy just sat behind the wheel watching his mate heave his stiff twenty five feet across?"

"Hold on..." Leyton thought it through. "There *is* something we're forgetting."

"The murder, or the castors the body had on underneath?"

"No, the three guys. You're right, silly me, it's all there. The 'Doer', the 'Driver', the 'Dragger'. Each assigned their separate duty."

To Garstone's muted comfort, she fully comprehended the situation... before putting another foot down over his account.

"It still means only two came along with the body, our assailant possibly neither."

"Bloody hell!" went Armitage, still buried inside the roundabout. "Like he actually heard us from down there...."

Garstone ducked under to where Armitage was sitting, closely touched by astonishment that his fellow DC had found something rather than just listening to a private conversation.

What both Leyton and him were shown passably resembled something from an old *Hammer Horror* movie. The chains holding the body flat were interconnected centrally, forming a sort of cross-like arrangement. Pulled to their limit, all four chain-ends converged below the man's waist, fixed tight to the bottom.

160

"So now do you believe me when I say 'planned professionally?'" Garstone referred it aside to Leyton.

"Looks very much that way. So-o-o our subject has torture on his agenda as well?"

The details indeed summed up to this being an expert's work, someone who'd obviously driven closely enough by to note both the roundabout and its structure. On this cue, Garstone couldn't help but throw a tricky one at her. Looking to make sure Armitage was still too busy to hear he motioned her away for total discretion.

"You don't reckon *Hargreaves* might have done this by any chance, do you, ma'am?" This made Leyton's face widen and he immediately made to retract the allegation. "Well at least possibly had a hand in it? Sorry, if that's a bridge too far, despite what else he's done today."

"The signs are there." Leyton went on pondering." but I hardly think he'd have time to organise it; *besides*, with the trouble he's in, he'd hardly be showing his face anywhere he knows us to be."

Not two seconds later than she'd spoken, a commotion erupted behind, at the gate. The roaring rectangular headlights of the Volvo forced their way through the five officers who'd tried there hardest to block it. A large hulking shape climbed out of the driver's side, heading straight for Leyton. Garstone shielded her as Hargreaves moved menacingly towards them.

"Thought I might find you around Totley somewhere," hissed the Superintendent.

He fixed his hardened look on Leyton, getting as close to her as Garstone tolerated.

"Just popping by to let you know you haven't heard the last of this. I'm going to destroy you, Leyton. And you too Garstone - if you've had any part in this devious trollop's scheme… you just make sure you sleep with the lights on!"

Looking at her with his fist held raised, all the way back to the car, Hargreaves effectively threw the other officers aside as climbed back in and drove away.

"Lunatic…." Leyton fumed "Maybe a little rich to say at the moment, I know, but all other words fail me."
"Aye, cracked enough to turn up at the scene of his own crime."
"Er, Greg, what have I just told you?" Leyton still didn't approve of his insistence that Hargreaves was a potential perpetrator. "However, before he does commit one - I think it's time we moved shop… that's hoping Leroy's finished the 'chain' game."

A near deafening crack, from metal striking a floor made everyone jump.

"That answer your question?" said Garstone, running back to the roundabout.
"Ey up, look at this!" his friend slid out, excitedly waving one of the chain ends.

(ii)

Armitage had stood in Sheffield's central mortuary, studying the chain end with bewilderment for the entire 15 minutes since arriving. With the threat ringing of a return from Hargreaves sooner rather than later, the detectives accepted Jamieson's crafty offer of using the main lab as an official continuation of the Totley School murder scene, cunningly combined into a

162

premature post-mortem to earn access.

A far more comfortable environment, though cooler (for obvious reasons), the large, newly refurbished main hall was welcoming and spacious, and despite the mounting body count a spare table existed to be found . Not like the old smell had gone with the old decor, the unbearable petrol-like stench supplied by foolishly un-lidded embalming fluids did not exactly make the new bright blue/grey combination work any better to stop Garstone clutching his nose all the time.

Laid on the back row alongside the two Donaldson brothers, all remaining signs of life in the still-anonymous new victim - provisionally named as 'No5' - had departed (the whiff maybe responsible). Around them, wondering up and down, Garstone, Jamison and his old friend, ageing senior pathologist Professor Euan FitzMichael made better use of time whilst waiting for Leyton to finally catch up.

FitzMichael was never a man short of things to moan over. The lanky Irish-Scottish housekeeper was nearer to retirement than his reasonably brown mop top testified, and wasn't willing to handle hunting for everything all over again, despite the shiny new cabinets being labelled more clearly than stringent. Every morning, day and evening he wove in and out round every single tray, inspecting the instruments to the point that anyone else in the room would suspect a case of OCD. Paranoid by his own admission that something had moved, regardless of there being a body on that particular table, he was a detective by his own merits, within this building. The last thing he still needed, right now was Leroy Armitage in his laboratory, the DC's disreputable clumsiness no less familiar to him than it was with Leyton.

"Will you put that bloody thing down?!" Garstone told his

wayward co-worker, finally running out of his patience "We're here to look at a body, not help you crack your chain puzzles."

"Just can't get over how it did that." Armitage made quite clear of having not listened to a word they'd explained back at the schoolyard.

"What sort of metal cracks its coat off like that… just don't get it?"

"Come on then, boys!" Leyton entered, rolling up her sleeves and sliding on the gloves. "I thought you'd have long made a start on things."

"You think I'd trust these two around a body, without proper adult supervision?" Jamison scoffed "DC Armitage gets confused by enough already."

"I'm supposed to be the confused one this evening, Don."

"I'm very glad to hear that." Jamison shifted the sheet back further for her divine attention. "Because there's plenty more for you where that came from."

As the pathologist revealed the now de-clothed body, Leyton studied it over aimlessly, totally unsure what she was meant to see.

"I never believed there to be a wound on the chest anywhere." she wondered why she was being shown like this.

"Well the visible chest injury reported is then either an impeccable fast-closer, or a very good trick-shop gift's had you going."

Adding his glasses, to appear mistaken rather than just hopeless at lying Jamison toured the upper chest beyond the right nipple. No even slight cut, entry or exit wound showed. As he looked back up over his octagonal frames at her, Leyton only hoped it was an after-effect of her earlier sanity exit.

"Have you got the victim's shirt handy?"

He asked Garstone who in response picked up a large packet and handed it to Leyton.

Hoisting out the bloodied magenta sweatshirt carefully, she laid it on a vacant table behind. Garstone was drawn to a small tear on the upper front, which he flicked curiously at. Leyton also perused the Y-shaped rip before he had chance to explain the find quite ably himself.

"Interesting." she stood back, silently ruminating the cause of a wound gap this big "Someone has *literally* made their mark this time." She took the pack of clothes again and rifled inside like a five year old child unwrapping her Christmas present. "I do happen to recall a collared layer beneath."

Leyton followed her answer up by laying a black polo shirt next to the sweater. They were both surprised to find this other garment completely undamaged, Impossible to trace even a slight incision in the shirt's fabric this usually vulnerable example of light-woven attire was fully intact, like some new breakthrough design in bulletproof vest.

"You don't suppose a badge could have fetched this sort of hole out, do you?"

Armitage lifted the sweater close, obviously enduring a serious level of condensation in his lenses. He knew what was coming from Leyton next so had to conjure up his next excuse for staring blankly at an important evidence item pretty sharpish.

"He must have been working for some sort of organisation, wi' a top like that on."
"Aye, would be a big one."

Garstone limited his answer to basics as he tried to bridge the line exactly between accepting Armitage's causally dashed appraisals, and totally dismissing them wholly to assuage Leyton.

"Like a *name-card thing - thick plastic* type?" he whispered "You can't rule it out ma'am. If someone pulled a badge off, aggressively it would hardly come off as cleanly as Will's tie, eh?"

(So, that moves us no closer to learning No5's real name yet.)
Leyton managed to restrict her agitation from reactivating to the more trivial of problems. Acting like some cookery student who'd just turned up to find the class cancelled, she reluctantly folded the shirts back into the packet.

"With the dental records unlikely to reach us tonight we might as well just get on with the rest of the entertainment."
"You seem in with chance of identifying the *perpetrator* sooner than the victim," Jamison dropped some news on them "Start at.... *male with somewhat ham-fisted skills in the use of his weapon.*"
"Tha still on about that?" whinged Armitage.
"Well, I can safely say that once you look at this beauty...." Jamison slowly turned the body face down, with reluctant help from FitzMichael. "I doubt you'll be finding time to talk about anything else for today."

With his left index, he cleared the back of 'No5's neck. The trauma Leyton saw now in front of her was indeed amongst the most impeccably created she'd ever noticed. Like a badly- drawn London Tube sign, the shape was a neat circular gash, about half an inch in diameter, a deep cut-line travelling through at a roughly horizontal angle.

"Christ on a chopper!" Garstone said, bemused. "What kind of machine could've done this?"

"Something the offender's obviously also been qualified to use legally," Leyton generalised.

Letting Jamison complete cleansing, she then arced her head to see the unusual laceration from a better angle, circling the table continuously.

"Then, crimes of convenience occur in many a way."
"Aye, summat nicked from work, probs," Armitage said, actually bothering to study before opening his mouth. "Snuck up behind and at the right moment...*thppt!*" he mimicked a 'raspberry' sound to complete it.
"And straight out again." Jamison rounded off the story as normal.
"How can you tell that by just looking at the shape?" said Garstone "Only the *boss* here would know that."
"It's quite easy, DC Garstone. Loosely aimed weapon, *tool - whatever* you insisted it was - applied rapidly, in the heat of the moment, just enough to cause the necessary damage, back out and off he goes."

He mimed with a pen, the route that the weapon would have most likely taken according to his arrogant judgement. The X-ray showed its route through the tissue perfectly well, as Leyton could see without Jamison's tutelage. The business end had been pushed in 'downhill' - just far enough to sever the windpipe considerably.

"Obviously our friend got it more to the left than to the right, shall we say, before he swiftly retracted it."
"Yuck..."
"Given the neat application, you'd be looking at the work of a power tool - the type involved comprising a spinning mechanism."

Garstone listened but more distantly, poring over the rest of the scar. The disappearance of the 'A' from the latest two scenes paled into second-placed significance. Their new model was a more contrived cut - reaching out to him like an evil eye, he had to fight off the possession to avoid being consumed as Leyton had been.

(Tell me something mate,) he rehearsed his next question for Jamison, *(if the cut was this clean, how did it manage to grow an additional slit, shooting about an inch out either side?)*

"Bring them over." Jamison asked him, a person very often able to hear thoughts out loud.

Garstone remembered where they were, almost dragging Jamison's coat off the table with them.

"Aw, me drink," moaned Armitage, seeing his water had also hit the deck.
"It's ok, I got it." Garstone rescued the cup. "Cheer up mate it's only water."

Too late - it had been said loud enough to fetch FitzMichael over. "*What's* only water?!" he cut sternly into the commotion "That better not be something out of one of my bottles; if so that's the last time you ever come in my lab."

Armitage grabbed a paper towel and got straight back.

"Here…" FitzMichael snatched it from him. "You wonder why there's no eating or drinking allowed in here? Looks like I'll have to include *tap water* in the policy from now on."

Garstone meantime was already beginning the second lap round, with the 'trail' then the 'tube sign' and back again, trying to balance the two visions like badly-overlapping internet screens.

"Did you actually take in anything new from that so-called in depth study, Gregg?"   Leyton asked as the photo came to her attention.

"Aye," He looked her in the eye as he supplemented his answer with extra words "I see where all that blood in the car park's from."

"Oh, yes - that which magically vanished from the roundabout, correct?" She borrowed both photos back. (*Hey, hold on....*)

Expectedly unconvinced by his trite ponderings, Leyton grabbed the whole envelope to find that it was a different collection in his grasp, reading *'Dore/Totley' 1-5'* on the pack. After having emptied all the pictures, and rowed them up on a whiteboard, unusually sloppily she made a tree placing photos of Ecclesby, McMahon and Peter Donaldson to one branch while Nigel and 'No5' sat independently alongside.

"Right, now we're organised, children, let's begin." Leyton enjoyed speaking to the DCs like infant school children when she knew their focus was irritatingly short.

 "So-o-o, either our mystery psychopath has a grudge on Bob Carolgees, or having so far took out five innocent people may be still yet to pounce on the right.... yes ok, thankyou..."

Leyton made Armitage an offer of discussing their children's TV memories in depth later at McGanlon's in return for his concentration on the here-and-now, before continuing. Inking a few small details below, relating as to how and where the various subjects had come to meet their maker, a pedal cycle atop a squiggly line had to suffice for Nigel's location.

"Right, apart from still missing our man's real name, anything else important we have neglected to cover at this point?"

She peered across the faces of both DCs for an answer - plus Jamison's if he could be at all bothered - then having given up swapped her green marker for a blue, stemming victims 1,2 and 3 to the 'A' and the swing.

"No? Right, as you're clearly having difficulty adjusting to the new lighting...."

Leyton trawled through marked likenesses of the three earlier crimes, circling the killer's fabled inscription, and then linked it to an empty bubble under 'Nigel'. Holding off for a moment, she ensured the lads were watching. Armitage seemed set to air his viewpoint but the wait came to nothing so she added another circle round 'Tube sign' - not that a wound of such shape really needed one.

"Don't think summat's quite right wi' that, ma'am." Armitage finally made her day.

Handing him the pen, she dared to value his point, a great wake-up call with her marbles only just returning to place. The logicality presented itself on the spot.

(For murders1 - 3, he uses a bladed implement for the 'A' thing, but not the actual killing. Vice versa: Nigel Donaldson's death is a purely blade-related despatch, YET slings it away into the bushes on departure, having not made any visible marks apart from those his own feet leave. Again, he'd used the same knife he'd carved the logo with; blood's now on the blade, forcing its immediate discard.)

Leyton put a question mark below the 'Nigel' circle. "A rather odd way round indeed, but falls into place at the end. Wouldn't you agree, Greg?"

170

Her gaze travelled across his shoulder to her other DC who she'd caught staring starboard once again. Garstone was actually distracted by the presence of a fourth person beside him - FitzMichael who with little better left to do for the evening had decided to join them. *(Not satisfied at inviting herself in with a body over her shoulder, she now uses my lab as a bloody briefing room.)*

"These have nothing so far in common with the fifth one, guys." he spoke to show where his attention still went, "You're probably right; why he ditched the Stanley..."
"Ahem, if you don't mind me squeezing in here for a second..." Jamison assumed FitzMichael would rather from him, than a couple of burbling detectives. "I might know *exactly* what DC Garstone's trying to get together for us."

Garstone surrendered the 'Tube' photo back, letting the pompous pathologist borrow the reins.

"Mmmm..." he re-familiarised with the shape but saw a difference this time. "We have a wound of two halves here, guys."

Leyton concluded the puncture had either swelled half a time its size, but looking closer, it wasn't so. The horizontal cut had a much-diminished visibility on the shot. Garstone retracted the photo from Jamison, smelling the sensation arising. *(It's definitely a cut to the outer tissue only - either a blade, or subsequent and possibly sudden impact. May have been accidental, even.)* He looked his DI in her eyeballs hoping this important penny had dropped. It quite obviously had, though it took another unassuming examination of the 'tube sign' to believe things.

171

I think we can make perfect sense of it now she thought, nearly out loud. *Murderer, or two accomplices should I say, load him into the back seat. The journey, from the actual scene of attack up to Totley is possibly brief but still sufficient to forget which way round the body was laid, when they finally arrive. First man opens the back door on his side ...OOPS its the legs he grabs first. Devoid of support at the other end, No5's head lands on the floor, obviously quite hard too. The immediate flesh area round the first wound would inevitably remain wet or weakened. Thus the head wobbles on impact, forcing the damaged flesh wider apart; blood comes rushing out once again.)*

"It all fits like a glove now Greg." said Leyton.
"About bloody time." FitzMichael disappointed her with the reason for his sudden happiness. "That means you can all go elsewhere at last, does it?"
"I don't think so, just yet..." Garstone asked her for the *Scene 5* envelope. "Without disrespect, ma'am...."

He trawled through them, aiming for a reasonably close take of his favourite, the 'wavy edge'.

"What now?" FitzMichael bleated.
"We may now have come up with an explanation for this ripple Gregg's so fascinated with." Leyton told him.
"It's nothing quite that complex." Jamison bounced their own volley of knowledge straight back at them.

(Similar to what Leyton just said, it was 'pumped' out by the head swinging from side to side. Such movement would repeatedly open and shut the hole like a blinking eye. Like it works on a newspaper press - pattern in movement causes pattern in print.)
Leyton had barely time to understand him before FitzMichael took her right the way.

"If that's not a footprint, I'm a Chinaman." he announced, silencing everyone with his sudden wisdom "'*Wave line*' indeed."

"Thanks." Garstone mumbled aside to his new assistant, glad someone had given him a break.

He arranged the three blood trail close-ups on the board, recreating the trail.

"That is way too finely cut for an incidental spill, blood or any other substance that'd be as runny." observed FitzMichael, a man who'd been round the block more times than anyone in the room, "Don, your camera a moment, please."

Obligingly, Jamison fished about underneath his coat, after his favourite toy. Leyton scrolled through the images until she found the three shots relevant. Zooming straight to the undulation, she passed it back to him, then in turn onto Garstone.

"Do you honestly think a blood trickle would form repetitions that accurate?"

She half-refilled Armitage's spilt cup then poured a trail of water along a vacant table to her left, shaking it side to side as she moved along. Enlarging the picture to the limit of pixel capability, Armitage could almost see what Garstone had been struggling to make him.

This pattern that had dominated her DC's evening was cut in, neither by altercations with the rough tarmac texture *or* by any experiment involving some possibly absurd-sized biscuit shaper: the edge of a shoe print could be just be distinguished in the ripple line. This crescent-ish indent, partnered with another, smaller became the giveaway. Garstone, on calculated support from FitzMichael filed his conclusion after an infinitely long time gazing at the shot.

"One… two three…." he measured the decoration, the prints set apart by a good yard. "The guy clearly intended to miss it, just had nowhere to dodge onto."

"Our prints denote the work of a large male shoe," Leyton continued only wanting his answer, less the subsequent rigmoral. "Likely to be at least an *11*."

"There's only a couple of them to look at - couple and a half did you say?" Armitage said, confusing Leyton as to whether it had sunk in.

"We did capture the trail in full, as required," Jamison denied any neglect "not just the portion that your DC's been wasting everyone's time with." (*All the action happened up one end of the pitch- it just looks like the fool turned off his floodlights too soon. Clever.*)

He returned to the first picture again.

"Quite likely you have someone with two right feet as opposed to two left."

"And still someone with no name, laying on the table in front of us …" Leyton reminded him of what still needed clearing up, "Oh, hello, found us have you?"

Leyton and her entire team turned away to greet PC Thompson, stood in the door with a shoebox tucked underarm, more than relieved to have finally got the right place.

"It took enough time." the younger cop laughed, "You swines had me drive all the way back to Midelson Road to find out where you were hiding!"

FitzMichael was happy for a record second time this evening:

The put-upon pathologist reserved a somewhat warmer reception for uniformed officers, sensing an air of discipline in the sight of their outfits that seemed to be lacking in a couple of cavalier detectives.

Thompson carried the box across, almost dropping it on seeing 'No5's body already lying there. He was amongst many not used to seeing a body only found two hours ago lying on a mortuary table.

"You look like you know this bloke, Will." Garstone joked at him.
"It would be good if someone did," said Leyton. "The colour of his shirt could still help us." (*That's one avenue we've neglected to explore*)

The PC found the sweater and laid it out, not taking long in establishing he was unlikely to bring anything useful to the table - aside from a selection of *No5*'s surviving belongings.

"You ok if I have a look?" Garstone butted his head in almost across her view line, practically defeating the point of Leyton opening out the shirt once more. "Hey, you noticed *that* yet?"

He picked away gingerly at the Y-tear again, spotting there the end of a large letter in gold, just above the rip. A rough shape could be traced in the spilt speckles of gold and white glitter.

"It's an 'A', alright!"
"It was, until someone rubbed it off," thought the DI, "though that's certainly where the abrasion came from."

(They'd taken No5's badge, along with anything containing his name or image, but that still left the source of identity engraved on his clothes also to lose. Not as quick to get rid of as a badge.)

"There's another letter - it got taken off good and proper, like."
Garstone provided her with another clue, which he then dashed in tandem.
"Looks possibly…hmm… a '*C*'?"

Leyton could pick out the overall curvature in the white scatter, forming a firework pattern together with the gold. As the shape solidified itself to her, it formed more of an 'S'.

"Do you mind if I took a peek for myself?" Jamison leant over, unable as ever to restrain his fascination for more than five minutes. "That, I think you'll discover is a '*Social Aid*' insignia you re looking at." he told them.

The shirt matched with the description of the charity's uniform right away to him (his wife had managed their Chesterfield road branch for the last thirteen years.) Leyton's face had now whitened horrifically, as if she'd just lost an argument with a magnesium flare. Hardly able to speak anymore, she shook her head slowly at the obliterated print.

"Were there any personal items that managed to stay with him?"
"Yes, his mobile, believe it or not." said Thompson, brightly.

The young PC opened the small box with N05's few surviving possessions. Only his belt and a near crumpled *Nokia* sat at the bottom, which Leyton impatiently snatched out, trying to activate.

"The battery's flat as a pancake though, no point even trying it."
"I've an old adaptor kicking about in the Vec' somewhere." Garstone helped, handing Leyton his car keys "Want to try your luck?"
"Thanks," Leyton whispered, not smiling as she turned for the

door.

The still vaguely doo-lalley DI nearly forgot where Garstone had parked, almost trying to climb into FitzMichael's black Citroen XM instead. Finally getting the right door, she barricaded herself inside the Vectra, fired the ignition and plugged in.

Luck being on her side, the mobile spluttered into activity, lighting up little differently to her own - apart from an Orange display welcoming her instead of her usual O2 one. As soon as the *menu* option arrived, she went straight to 'Events' and checked over 'No5's diary from the last seven days this month.

"October...October...here we go....FRI 21 - Weston Park museum trip (afternoon)... SAT 22 - Match, home vs. Bradford... SUN 23 - blank... MON 24 - Robbie's mum's, nine thirt..."

Leyton dropped the phone onto her lap, letting it slide off into the footwell. Please let this be a mistake, she thought to herself, holding back the temptation to cry as she knew something wasn't right.

9

HURTS OF THE JOB

(i)

"I hope I'm doing the right thing here, Greg." Leyton repeated for the fourth time. She was aiming short on talk, trying to concentrate as that obscured turn-off in the middle of Dore loomed once again.

"It's best he knows soon as possible, ma'am."
Garstone stole the quickest way he could into justifying their proposed drop in on the Draycott household at seven o'clock in the morning.

To Leyton, it felt like calling round to visit Count Dracula whilst on a milk round today; the circumstances of the journey made her spine vibrate with the same degree of dread. Even though she knew Robbie did not work weekends, the startling entry on the fifth victim's visiting schedules needed clearing.

The DI became visibly unsettled as her colleague slowed the Vectra along the kerb on Highcroft Close. Looking to make sure he'd not overshot the house, Garstone nearly then did, catching her at it again. Totally believing it his fault this time, he sympathised with her judgement

"You want to leave it a few minutes, before going 'under'?" he asked, softly.
"I can't wait in a car, all day, Greg. I'm just going to count one-to-five, and dive."
"Okay" he opened the car door, grabbing his coat. "You lead, I'll

follow."

"No disrespect intended," Leyton stopped him" but I'd rather face the consequences alone. I just don't want you to open your mouth and come out with…well, you know… the wrong thing."

"Aye, it's ok."

Garstone threw his jacket back on the seat, struggling to be assured that she was prepared to go ahead with this most delicate of visits. He still had to stay out here on 'sentry duty' - if Hargreaves possessed enough gall to pull that stunt in Totley last night, there was little boundary to how far his revenge would extend. Leyton already opened that familiar can of worms before he could get it on the table.

"That's also an issue." she insisted "Get Leroy or Will up straight here as well."

"Er, ma'am…"

"That's an order, Greg. I'd not actually forgotten while in cloud cuckoo world, that we have an extremely vulnerable, traumatised young man inside that house. On top of which, Hargreaves will be undeterred by the prospect of his job going permanently down the toilet, if *so* desperate for his own back."

"Okay, fine." Garstone climbed back in "Just promise me one thing, ma'am. The moment he looks like not taking it well, get the hell back out of there."

"I'll do my job, Greg." she admonished, not prepared to be questioned, "I've got two people's to do now, after all." She climbed out and walked through the gate.

"By the way," Garstone called out after her. "It's 'cloud cuckoo *land*', not 'world'."

Leyton looked back and smirked softly at his cockiness before turning to tackle the hardest part of the morning… or possibly her career. (*Sod it; I might as well dive in face first.*) She

179

completed the first step of the journey, down the drive slowly leaning her thumb on the bell while anticipating the hell Barbara might be shortly opening her door to. Hearing the buzzer, Leyton released held her finger unaware she'd held it down for nearly eight seconds. With the point of no return passed, she listened out for Barbara's footsteps. (*Here go-oes*)

The bolt slid, the chain went back. Judging by her fearless opening of the door, Barbara Draycott did however expect it to be Midelson Rd personnel visiting.

"Jo...." she welcomed her, "How are you? I thought I recognised that voice outside."
"Ah, that's touching of you." Leyton laughed, trying to bury the more serious issue for now, "I take it you don't get many southerners in the village."
"Would you like to come in? I know it's very early - but while Robbie's out of the way..."

She peered through the lounge window, at the car outside.

"Would DC...*Armitage* is it, like to join you as well? He's most welcome."
"He's not here today, I'm afraid. That's DC Garstone in the car."
"Has he got to stay out there in the freezing cold while you're inside enjoying a coffee?"
"I'm, afraid so. If you want to send one out to Greg though, it won't be wasted. He'll have white with two sugars."
"Certainly."

Barbara smiled and topped up for a third mug full then recommenced boiling. Leyton meanwhile strode across the lounge and budged the curtain a little apart, to ensure Garstone was staying out of mischief.

"He could always come inside and have it." Barbara insisted, "DC Armitage will remember the address if he also shows."

"We can't take chances at the moment. What DCS Hargreaves did to your son's serious enough, without the possible repercussions our department may face."

"Superintendent Hargreaves?"

Barbara dropped her jaw open as if she'd just witnessed a national scandal unfolding right in front of her, not that she was that far off the mark.

"Yes, that lovely man who helped himself to your son, sans warrant, yesterday morning." Leyton let Barbara take it in for a moment before continuing.

"The other problem is he hasn't seemed so far prepared to take his punishment hands down, after I reported him."

"Gosh, turning in a superior officer takes some stamina."

"And stupidity." Leyton ducked her head in a modest effort to downplay her sin "He even paid us a jolly old visit at our latest murder scene to inform us he know who'd squealed."

"Yes, I heard there'd been a fifth one."

(Oh, shit, no way out of it - it's now or never.)

Leyton found herself placed back at the task in hand, one that was going to require a standard of diplomacy behind even her impeccable levels. She unzipped her handbag, sliding out the envelope marked 'No5' plus various smaller-printed formalities from the forensic staff.

"Is this the person you found at the school last night?" asked Barbara, watching Leyton unfold the single photo for her attention.

"Yes, I'm afraid so," she handed Barbara the picture "although

181

his identity's still awaiting conformation. We hope you might be able to help towards saving us the trouble."

"Oh, my...my g..."

Barbara's face whitened with dread, as she looked very closely, briefly at the picture, then up at the DI. She sounded faint as she reached for her glasses case.

(Here we go then - best of luck, Joanne.)

"I take it you know who it is then?" said Leyton, shakily

"I must say that I do, Jo. It...it...it's Jon..."

"Might it be Jon Clougton, if you are struggling to remember?"

"Yes."

"They returned that as his supposed identity this morning. Believed to be an employee of Social Aid, a Sheffield care trust, funded by the NHS."

"I don't need that many details." Barbara fought back a tearful breakdown by short margins. "He was like a dad to my Robbie - even more of one than his *real* father."

Leyton allowed her to reassume her nerves before asking the next item, going in carefully as Barbara studied the image sitting in her palm. Robbie's mum began to shake, as though she'd just seen someone's world crashing down. Comfortable now that she'd got the dropping of the first bomb over, Leyton got her notepad out and sat back down as Barbara fetched her coffee in.

"If you can verify that the deceased matches with the name, I'll be able to break the tragic news to Robbie, tough as I find having to do so."

"Can't you find possibly another way round it?" pleaded Barbara. "Pretend that Jon's gone away, even?"

"He'll have to know sometime: I will break it sensitively to him, as procedure requires. Meanwhile, has he got any other father figures - role models as such?"

182

"Only Ray, the gentleman he works for. Why?"

Leyton sensed this was risky and *not* because she was asking Barbara something she already knew herself. She picked up her cup casually for a long savouring slurp, maintaining eye contact for Barbara's assurance.

"I've heard a lot about Ray too, not one word of it bad."
"Robbie worships the very ground that man walks on. It's hard to tell who he looks up to most, sometimes."
"Competition is often a deadly thing."
"Jon was gay, if you're interested in knowing."
"Yes, now you come to mention it. It proved useful to understand that Mr Gipton *also* bats for the other side."
"He never told me that. I thought Robbie would have probably let it slip, ages back."
"A boy well-schooled in the act of discretion." Leyton exclaimed in salutary tones as she picked up another biscuit. "Only, your son was nettled into it, very likely."
"Are you trying to say there's an actual hate campaign out there, targeting my lad?"
"I would so hate to, but both have been subject to prejudice-related violence in the past. Robbie, with being labelled 'different' is unfortunately the most liable target."

Leyton stopped to scribble down what she could catch of the conversation, waiting for Barbara to calm down. Attacking her coffee once again, she spoke.

"I'm sorry if all this sounds a weight to drop on you, but it is paramount that we learn all we can, in order to know whether our suspect operates to a pattern."
"Robbie has taken some hell since he became…what he is now." Barbara was back in full voice again, battling the stress of the situation with her remaining courage. "A load of lads who gather

outside the shops…'Chavs', I believe, nowadays. They often wear caps and big necklace type things… I can't begin to describe the language I normally hear them use as I go into the shop."

"Would a youth called Danny Bennington fit such description?" Leyton used the only other available name.

(How can HE have done it, Jo, you stupid moo, that lad can't punch his way through a wet paper bag. He's all talk and no action…. Not to mention in pain from a rather nasty altercation with someone's Ford Focus recently.) She allowed the can of worms to open, Barbara helping to pour them out for her.

"That spiteful little Bennington wretch is the reason my Robbie has to get a lift everywhere, even just to go round the corner. I suppose then a lot of kids in the estate are little different; you only have to bat an eye at them and you get a mouthful of…."

"'ELLO-O-O…" came a cheery young male voice from behind them. The door swung open and Robbie plodded in.

"Oh, hi Robbie," said Leyton, "Sorry if we woke you."

"It's OK, Jo. How are you doing?"

"I think she prefers to be called DI Leyton, dear." Barbara corrected him,

"Sensitive people deserve star treatment." Leyton grinned.

"Star? Is that what I am?" Robbie brightened up. "No one's ever called me that before."

He bounced about in merriment. Leyton patiently waited for him to calm as she rehearsed to herself the difficult news she was about to break.

"Why don't you sit down, Rob?" offered Barbara, dragging a seat up. "Jo's got something she wants to tell you."

Leyton, finding the door had been fully opened for her now, took a deep breath, looking down at her coffee, and then faced them both.

(ii)

The hands-free in Armitage's car sounded its almost unbearable signature as the DC tried to show for once, that he was less distracted behind the wheel than his colleagues believed. He knew Garstone was not going to stop till he got an answer, however and finally decided to take the call as he pulled up behind a queue coming into Dore.

"Sorry mate," Armitage looked quickly for a lie "Traffic at Parkhead were a bastard." Won't be a tic."
"Where are you now?" Garstone asked, unconcerned.
"In Dore. Just turning up by that grocers' place. Almost with you."
"Could do with staying clear at the mo', Le…. (*Oh, god, too late*.)"

Garstone heard a car motor nearby and looked back to see a red Ford vehicle cruising up the street.

"Ayup," Armitage pulled over, "Too late, now, eh?"
"Get back, mate!" Garstone leapt out to stop him. "Stop inside if you can."

Before he had chance to ask why, Leyton and Barbara both came dashing out of the door and up the drive towards them.

"What the hell…" Garstone tried to find out.
"I'd duck for cover, if I were you, boys!" Leyton stopped both of her men "I may have made a bit of a misjudgement in my

delivery."

The volume of Leyton's 'mistake' turned its own dial up as chaotic strings of banging and smashing came from inside. The front curtain was now lying on the lounge floor, revealing the carnage that had been Barbara's pretty little lounge only moments earlier. A cup came flying at the window from inside, followed shortly after by terrible demented hollering.

"WAAAAAAAAAAAAHH!!! AAAAAAAAAAAAHHHHHHHHH!!! NO-O-O-O! WAAAA-H-H-AAAAAHHH!!!"

Robbie picked up the small wooden chair from the corner of the room, which had once been his Gran's. Leyton restrained his mum again from approaching as he hurled it through the pane.

"Rob…Rob darling, please stop…"

Barbara cried in Leyton's arms, ignoring the fact that the chair had landed, in one piece on the garden rockery. As she comforted her, Leyton felt rather small from not reading the signs earlier. The noise inside continued, though now less smashes, instead more the sound of doors within the house taking a splintering kick. Only the moment Garstone and Armitage rose from behind the car, did Leyton decide it was a vague fraction safer to approach the youngster. Signalling the others to stay with Barbara, she crept slowly down the drive, and nudged the back door slightly open.

"Robbie…" she called inside, "It's Jo! Where are you?"

She got her reply from a vase flying through the hallway.

"Go away! He's dead! Leave me!" screamed Robbie. "My friend is dead! Jon is dead! Someone murdered my friend! He's dead!

DEAD! *DE-E-E-E-A-A-D*!!!!"

Leyton crossed into the dining room in time to find Robbie swooping up a plate from the dresser. She dived for cover yet again as he hurled it aimlessly, before deciding now wasn't quite yet the time to bother him. Ducking all the way back through the kitchen, she made it out again, running almost straight into Armitage.

"Don't risk it, Leroy! Low-flying crockery does tend to hurt, whatever your build!"
"Will's just on his way," shouted Garstone, "Gonna be about three minutes."
"Best leave Robbie to it in that case," said Armitage, "He'll finally end up running out of stuff to break, you watch him."

Leyton agreed, retreating back to the pavement with the others. Robbie eventually sounded like he'd got bored of his hissy-fit, though no one amongst the three officers, or Barbara, seemed keen on pushing their luck again. Before it even crossed Leyton's mind to retry the stunt, sirens sounded as a recognised unit stormed down the street to join the gathering. Thompson and his team jumped out, Leyton pointing them down the drive.

"You two in through the front," PC Hall instructed, making for the kitchen side, to cut Robbie off.

A huge catastrophe of noise and screams started over again as all three, including Raylesthorpe, cornered the boy to restrain him. His mother joined in the noise now, screaming as he was hauled out in a brutal police armlock.

"NO-O-O-O!" she cried, trying to run towards the officers.
"Back, love, he'll be ok in a bit." Armitage stopped her, "Won't hurt him, will we ma'am…Ma'am…?"

187

He looked round to see Leyton had disappeared. Garstone, noticing she'd got back in the car, could understand as he himself felt a lump from witnessing the distressing scene behind.

Garstone felt a quake in his boots over approaching the Midelson canteen, for the whole rest of the Saturday shift. Having had a brief lunch at home, solely to stay out of Leyton's way, the lure of a late afternoon snack before heading back for the Halloween dress night in Totley became no longer resistible. He'd stayed laid low in his office since getting back in at about one o'clock, to deal with all the papers she'd seemed too upset to handle, so finally had to break from his restraints.

"Where you heading off to, Ivor-the-Skiver?" He caught Armitage also grabbing his jacket and car key. "Think we're also gonna end up falling out, stuck in here another two minutes?"
"Eh, no…" chuckled Armitage, shiftily, "Just summat to go grab for later. A good job them garden centres hold stuff back for people, eh?"
"Aye, whatever, just go for it, whilst she's out of the place."

Ignoring a strange look from his friend as he left, halfway into his jacket, Garstone was innocent enough of worry to smile properly at Raymond on his way past to the canteen. Catching Thompson deciding unhurriedly over his flavour of spring water from the slot machine, he smiled again stepping through the door, the PC not exactly interested as he searched himself for change making up the required £1.40

Garstone's naivety came to nothing the moment he walked in. There she was - DI Joanne Leyton sat there in all here charcoal-garbed glory, four tables along at the front. Getting past the till without a tap on his shoulder was not to happen so he manned up just enough to give her one instead and get it over with. As he took hold of the vacant chair opposite, Leyton unexpectedly warmed to his appearance, sliding her coffee aside. He caught a startling aroma as he sat.

"Cappuccino?" he judged it, amazed.
"Strong coffee might just make a strong cop once more…. Hopefully." Leyton discharged a blissfully glib explanation.
"Aye, right."
Garstone slunk back in his seat, glad something was seeing to it if the room's relaxing oak and orange redesign had disappointed already.

"Guessin' Leroy's been in for a cup sometime this morning, then."
"Eh?"
"I left the paper work in his capable hands while I looking for you."
"Christ Greg, we've only just shed one negligent detective from our department- do we need another right away?"

Turning heads with the raised voice turned Leyton's aside to gather her nerves before they had chance to dramatically elude her yet again. Garstone took this as a chance meanwhile to chase up that late afternoon lunch. Leaving his jacket to assure her he intended stopping, he swooped straight round to the hot counter intent on bagging the surviving lasagne, his prize for which being allowed to take the porcelain serving dish to enjoy it from. Ethel, behind the counter, long past asking what was wrong with using a plate instead carried it over to the table, allowing him to pay. Plonking himself back down over it, he hoped Leyton's envy at the gorgeous smell would generate a fresh subject to moan about, but again it was not to be.

"It must have been something I said."

189

"Strange - you did deliver the news in your normal diplomatic style, eh?"

"No, absolutely nothing - as you said, I performed the lines totally by the script."

Garstone laughed, nearly inhaling his next mouthful of minced beef and cheese up his nose by accident.

"What?" Leyton waited for him to come out with the joke she didn't see.

"Ah, nothing, seriously. Was just thinking', like... when informing someone of a person's death, we do still tell them the time and place we found him, correct?"

 "Some of the time."

"You don't think you may have come out with the 'dreaded' expression?"

"Round and round?" Leyton almost laughed as well "I assure you I avoided that, at every cost imaginable."

"Or anything sounding like it?"

"Like..."

"Well... where the body showed up.... On a *round...a...bout*?"

"Well, malapropisms can easily get out sometimes..." Leyton slowly gripped a shaky feeling. "Robbie could have...you know..."

"Aye, misheard it. Round-a-bout...round-and-round - the vowel match is the same...rest... not far off."

Quivering on the hand lowering her cup back down, the vibration was supplied by the reality of her minor incompetence. Matching Robbie's two tantrums side-by-side for their hefty similarities, the key one dominated. 'Round and Round', the audible echo of the vowels sitting in her hand.

"My exact words to Mrs Draycott - we discovered the victim spinning round on a roundabout."

190

Her sidekick had got it nailed indeed; still she had to try it out on her own piano as usual. Garstone dimmed his eyes, struggling with it.

"Round on a round-a-bout." Leyton pushed it at him for clarity. "Round on a *round and round*."

"Aye, you've got a groove." He had also started in with the lip-synch by now. "Could be 'round and round and round', even. That'd really light the kid's touch paper, no prob."
"I could have got away with blaming the swings again, instead."
"No, you're way best off telling the truth right away, ma'am. They'll soon hear from the news what they didn't hear from you, heh heh."
"Some people can't handle it either way, I suppose." Leyton supped her remaining drops, while eyeing Garstone's final fork-load going down. "Robbie wouldn't even be able to understand the difference in spelling, that's the problem."

She sunk back into her hands, forced to dwell on how the clocks might benefit from being turned back a day. This silence became so unbearable her DC put his fork down. Even without a repeat of her flip at the Plough, he never enjoyed seeing his boss like this. A mobile ringtone restrained him from asking, just at the second he puckered.

"You found her yet?" went Armitage, inquisitively.
"Aye, been sitting, taunting her with my dinner the last quarter an hour. I take it you've returned?"

He noticed Leyton holding her hand out, and passed it over. A couple of seconds later, Armitage was seen escorting her out to his Focus.

"So what have you got then?"

"Nowt else on that but there's something in the boot I thought you'd like for tonight."

"Go on then, what…"

Seeing she was still up to being a sport, Armitage led Leyton to the back of the Focus, and ordered her to close her eyes.

(iii)

Leyton was not a fan of looking at her own pretty face in the mirror but as she had the comfort of it being hidden behind a latex Madame Blackwidow mask tonight, the uneasiness diminished.

'Come on, you can do it', were amongst the more polite things Leyton mumbled as she remonstrated with the waist of her witch's dress. Resplendent with its smatters of fluorescent green 'slime', Armitage had reluctantly tailored it to fit without the need to remove her own garments. She felt behind for the Velcro link that held the outfit together round her but ultimately opted to leave her own cream jumper on show rather than risk her shoulder ligaments.

"'Ey, you giving us a twirl then, or what?" came a voice through the door behind her.

"Just the chap I need." This was actually the only time Leyton ever welcomed a man in the ladies' side without the need to arrest him "Do you mind stepping in here a minute?"

(My lucky day is it?) Armitage's glasses nearly fell off, though it was his ears that deceived him more.

"God you look sexy in that costume... hey you're could do wi' a bit of help at the back there."

"Yes, why else do you think I've appreciated you straying into the wrong side."

Armitage's face sunk as he realised a beyond-limits look at the most attractive detective in Sheffield was denied him once again catching a peep of her jumper protruding at the rear. Trying to avenge his loss, he applied the velcro loosely with a slight hesitation, hoping that it would later pop undone in full view of the full pub."

"Okay," he grinned, "lets go out and impress the gents."

He opened the door and ushered her out, following furtively with hope that fellow officers and pubgoers alike would recognise his trip to the ladies as purely 'police business.'

"*Woo-hoo-oo-oo...* so who's this scary old woman after with her stick tonight, then?"

Garstone took admiration to the witch that had suddenly landed in front of him without the aid of a broomstick.

"Pity about the face." he naturally twisted his own compliment at the end.

"Well I know you can't see my real one, Greg, but its not far off at the moment in terms of expression."

"Come on, we're supposed to be having a celebration...." Armitage tried his hand at amusing her. "We've found the leads, remember."

"Plenty, I'll give you that. Just possibly NOT connected to all the right collars."

(Possibly did- very possibly, but 'possibly's never 100%.)

"We're satisfied there were *two* lads - one in a car, the other legging it like Linford behind him."

He could detect on Leyton that she was content with the theory for now although the alarmingly sporadic of footprints at the stunt-course scene continued, deep inside to confuse.

"What… oh, aye, I get it, so you saying that Long John Silver may be the culprit?"
"Well I'd agree a wooden crutch wouldn't leave as many full-sized prints…er, hello?"
She looked over Armitage's shoulder to the tall figure dressed in pirate garb. "Can we help?"
"Sorry mate," Armitage put up his hand to signal all was meant well "Wasn't you we were on about."

Seeing their fellow pub-goer had even included a wooden leg in his efforts Garstone realised how they'd attracted his attention. The 'pirate', one of the gaggle of rowdy upper-sixths that frequented the place weekly, backed away saying nothing. His guilty gesture as he dissolved back amongst his fellow bar mates by-passed Leyton, who took admiring views of the authentic resemblance.

"I don't exactly spot the Halloween connection" she lightened up. "It's still pretty cool, all the same."
"Aye. Still beats sense what some do come in, eh?" Armitage grinned, reaching for his pint of Wards. "You get some right 'uns in these village pubs."
"You mean like a kid who's just come in, dressed slap-identical to all the guys we've scraped off the playground floor this week?" Garstone disturbed the issue with a suddenly different take.

Leyton, noticing him looking past her at someone other than a

194

pirate, had to remove the mask to make sure her vision wasn't as severely damaged as she gave to thinking. (*A lad who comes in wearing a red sweatshirt, moustache and a very badly adjusted wig on his....*)

Sure enough the image matched the one her cohort had just listed but it could be just coincidental - there were one or two hundred popular comedy icons doing the rounds that this other young man, could be mocking. Not that they had the same blotchy left upper cheek of the youngster facing right towards her, through a gap in the packed confines of the room, who instantly backed away on making eye contact.

"Danny Bennington, you little b…"

Leyton tried to give chase through the congested upper bar but Danny had the upper hand, already five feet from the door; she was stuck at about twenty with almost as many people in her way whichever exit she aimed for.

"Greg, stop him!"
"I've got a better way." Garstone pointed her back the other way "It's called a car."

A quick flash of a police badge was enough to clear them a passage to the top door within seconds. The duo both piled through the passenger side of the Vectra, Garstone inserting himself behind the wheel. Seatbelts the least of their concerns, they launched out left, going for the crossroads.

Garstone put the brakes on halfway over the colourful paved junction, though it was not because of a *Give Way* sign he'd just missed.

"Which way, Captain?"

"He would been mad to have retreated down a main road, thinking he can hide behind a Tesco Express all night."
"That only means *straight across* then…."

He volleyed across onto Hillfoot Road, and down into the precariously inclined S-bend only for to feel Leyton's tug on his elbow once again.

"There's his escape." She pointed out a 'public footpath' placard.
"I've got a go-o-o-d idea as to where *that* magic trail will take me."
"Had a bet on you saying that. You want me to come along?"
"No, you shoot on down to the bottom: make a blockade - Danny'll then have to decide between our handcuffs or a night crashing amongst cowpats."
"Okay."
"And grab Leroy too; with the tricks Danny Bennington normally has in store, we need to consider all options."

Garstone resumed his journey to take position, as Leyton meanwhile diverged on foot down the side lane. Her murky, unlit cut through the upper backbone of the village carried her through a tree-tunnelled gennel out onto the hill above Penny Lane itself. A sulphur whiff halted her over a small scorched tube in the leaves. (*Are people this desperate to set fireworks off illegally?*) Leaving the '*Traffic Light Fountain*' hidden from harm's way Leyton found herself looking into the valley below, from a scarcely visible brick path. Lights from the cottages she left above were all she had to guide her plus the few at the bottom belonging to the Cricket Inn. Spreading her legs wide, she resorted to a silly walk to steady herself on the mud, yet maintain some pace. As the route came to a sudden right, two-thirds down a short figure could be seen emerging at the end, turning to look back up at her.

The chiselly young face remained unmistakable, in the glow given off by the lights from a nearby pub.

"Get back here you f..."

Leaving the sentence incomplete for that glorious moment she'd finally land on him, Leyton erupted into pursuit once again. Her acceleration was a potential degree better than Bennington's own, with the flimsy old wooden bridge at the bottom having hopefully proved a slight delay.

She'd spotted this 'obstacle' when leaving Ray's garage on Thursday - thinking about it now it *had* to be the end of this same path. All Danny had to do was trip over into it, whilst foolishly looking behind himself and she'd be able to bring the net down.

A passing tug on her clothes suddenly yanked her with a torturing rip. Almost pulled right to the floor, she felt her finger catch on something steel, and pretty sharp with it. *(Why do I always forget there might be a barbed wire fence somewhere along the journey?)*

Trapped in her tracks, she wrestled aside near collapsed fence before accepting that the fruits, of two minutes of Armitage's 'precision' tailoring, required sacrifice. Yanking the velcro apart so hard it came off all on one half, she resumed the chase but the mishap had given Danny a vital gap of opportunity.

Leyton still remembered footsteps ratting over something solid right at the bottom so knew to expect the bridge. Taking a wild leap she cleared the worn six-foot planks in a single step.

Her point of entry onto Penny Lane brought her up against the toughest decision - Danny could have just as likely turned left as he could right. There was another Halloween party evidently in progress, at the Cricket Inn immediately to her left.

Visible round the side, a gathering enjoying the cold air of the beer garden passed up no sight of Bennington. Drawing her attention to the right, a car disappeared towards the bottom junction, keeping its side of the white lines without any avoiding swerves for possible human obstacles. Leyton listened out as it slowed out of sight, without any use of hooter.

He couldn't have got that far along, surely. But no more likely could he have attained a haven deep amongst the clientele of the Cricket Inn without his furtive behaviour arousing suspicion.

It turned spontaneously hopeless. Danny had all but vanished into thin air since she'd last seen a trace of his scrawny form disappearing across the bridge.

Only a hasty reunion with Garstone was left that could enable her cause. She reached inside for her phone - an instrument she'd had more than enough of today- ready to give him and Armitage their respective nudges. Flinging her fingers away at the keypad, she'd got up to *0789 455 when* the sound of a barking dog could be heard, not significantly loud as such but enough to make her miss her aim, entering '*0*#*' instead of the rest.

Quickly clearing the number before accidentally ringing it, she listened again for the sake of certainty. The barks repeated from exactly the same remote direction. Drawn to explore what lay across the road, she pushed the phone inside and let her instinct conduct her.

(iv)

Leyton catapulted through the woods, skipping the treacherous drive that Garstone had forced his Vectra along on Thursday. Bounding across long-fallen logs, stumps and the moss-ridden rocks that also peeped from the weeds she saw the lights of the farmhouses come closer.

Another noise, a crackling was just possible to hear but extremely faint, totally out-phased by the barks.

Leyton had heard plenty. That farmyard dog had cornered Danny. Once she could establish this as the cause of the noise, it took her just to issue the go-ahead and the little hoodlum was out of places to run. (*Providing Leroy also dives right in on the dot, the kennel remains his only hidey-hole.*)

(*Hold on…*)

Next thing she knew, the barking had stopped, replaced by something less excited-sounding. A pair of pathetic squeals suspended Leyton's chase. Crouching behind gorse, she couldn't hear the animal any longer but the 'crackling' sound was easier to decode. Against the cottages' shimmering porch lights, a figure moved. The silhouette had long vanished by the time she'd reached the fence. Twisting herself between the slats, she managed to emerge vertically on the other side, only then spoiling it as she tripped over an unseen lump in the yard.

She felt down and found fur. Making out the shape of a dog's head, her hands came across a patch of red leaking from somewhere. The shining burgundy-clad handle of a Swiss army knife peeped up from the back of its neck.

Sickened as ever at the killing of an animal, and letting the sight get to her for two long seconds, Leyton turned to where the 'crackling' was still audible. Louder, doubly distinct by this stage - what was more, it came right from the direction of no1 Tall Trees Farm itself.

Ray's garage door was found already positioned ajar as she arrived there, only a good foot maybe though Bennington, given his skinny build would have got in through half that gap.

The noise was far easier than ever to identify here. Music! Leyton vividly remembered one of his various eighties glam metal tapes roaring away on that battered old portable stereo, the last time she'd dropped in on his domain. (*Gosh Ray's on a late one tonight*)

The music faded to dead air for two seconds. Another track then began but the gap was enough to hear the clatter of tools hitting the floor somewhere at the back. A crashing that repeated filled out by a series of voices and what didn't seem too friendly a conversation going on, judging by the near-rhythmical amount of four-letter words she could make out.

"Let him go Ray!" She thrust out her famous leather-clad crest on encountering the source of chaos.

In a clearing at the back of the shop, likely vacated by a collected vehicle, Ray staggered to face her, keeping Danny Bennington in a painfully clumsy armlock. Leyton's eyes hardened at sight of a familiar yellow implement in the mechanic's hold, the shinier end pressed firmly against the boy's face.

"He broke into my property - why should I?" protested Ray "I've a right to protect it haven't I - unless you'd prefer to admit you're all for protecting the criminal?"

The encounter landed her with a humdinger of a tough decision, arresting *Ray* - a hereinto harmless, timid gentleman- on suspicion of murder and possession of an offensive weapon, or Bennington himself, for murdering a *dog*, trespass… and the headache he'd caused her the last four days.

The two of them looked up icily at her, but didn't speak further, not that Danny found it too easy anyway.

"Doesn't that knife, alone point the finger at you Ray?" Leyton spelled it out, softly but firmly "An identical tool was discovered near Mr Donaldson's body yesterday morning, having presumably been used to tear his throat open."

He could never seriously expect an officer, of Joanne Leyton's resourcefulness to believe this a coincidence - not least with that sixteen-piece set of ProtoCut's finest sitting on his wall, all contents of which bore the same impeccable resemblance.

The mechanic continued linking eyeballs with Leyton but said nothing further. His face acquired a highly unsettled expression, as if now reading a motive more sinister.

"Well, go on," Leyton shunted her persuasion along further but kept up the subtlety. "One of you has got something you're aching   to   tell!   Who's   first?"

10

GOING FOURTH AND MULTIPLIED

(i)

Everything had shot by in a blurred mess, this last fifteen hours. Leyton had barely any sign of where the void, she'd been unceremoniously thrust into might be leading. Very little could she remember apart from constant brightening and fading of the white/grey surroundings, with voices that came and went in competition. The last clear thing she could recollect before taking a sudden unseen blow to the back of her skull was two people grappling round on the floor in some dusty old garage, one with a certain tool in his grasp.

Leyton kept on going back there every time the other colours faded. Like a time loop was now set in motion - one from which she could not break - she waited for a further collision of colour, and the other voices she heard with it to return and rescue her, but everything seemed inflexible, stuck within its own repetitive picture.

The two-man scrum of Bennington versus Gipton continued in front of her, the words reciting themselves along. Another voice started to float within the room now as well... one that called to her.

"Joanne."

Louder plus slightly manlier sounding than the first time, someone else was here, someone who could get her out. She turned to her right and as so the colour turned too, departing the gloomy rustiness of Ray Gipton's garage interior for a clearer blueish-white air, but only until obscured by a new shape looming over her closely... *a tall human one.*

A face appeared, one uncannily resembling DC Garstone's.

Everything lit up around her as she thrust herself off the deep pillow she found herself lying against. Taking in the scene, she was now in a tiny room, facing a corrugated sea-green curtain.

"Don't you know you shouldn't shout in hospitals?" were her first words to welcome her bedside visitor.
Realising her rudeness, she sunk back on her pillow
"So correct me, it's sometime on Sunday, October 30th, now is it?"
"Aye, about 10 past 10 in the morning, in case you're still too out for times and dates." That's one hell of a sleep that you had, thought you were as much a goner as Bennington when we got to you."
"Oh, ho- ho."
"No, 'goner', I said. Danny's dead."
"What?"

Before he knew it, Garstone was dropped right at the position of explaining to Leyton how he'd found Ray and her lying on the shop floor, while Armitage, Thompson and the lads discovered Danny Bennington in the toilet at the back, dangling off a wall-hook by the chain stolen from the garage shutter. Still she took it with less shock than expected.

"I can only narrow it down to one simple conclusion at this stage, Greg."
"I'm all ears...."
"Danny did it."
"To who?" Garstone now showed himself to be slow off the

mark.

"That'll be the victims and his good self."

"You've only been awake three minutes and you already know everything, or at least guess so."

"There was no one else in the room at the time." Leyton laid it out for him.

He knocked both Ray and I out cold. After watching us go down and not look like getting up again he obviously believed he'd taken it the distance.

"Knowing he'd be discovered in a room, surrounded by items matching the very same used in a murder one day earlier, he did the one honourable thing."

"Aye, I get it - gave the story a kind of Romeo and Juliet ending But why?"

"He had plenty to lose."

Truth be remembered rightly, Bennington had only recorded one spot of trouble with the law so far - that which she already knew of, first hand. He'd kept it, plus his recent predicament in Dore quiet from his employer, but this new harsher encounter with the law would unveil it dangerously sooner.

"Kid gets sacked even if found innocent, yeah?"

"Well you ought to foresee the verdict, as it was you who did the tidying up."

"You actually came round when I first found you."

Not that she'd have known, judging the gobbledygook she was spouting, it couldn't have been Garstone that Leyton thought she was chatting to. She didn't really desire to be reminded of having been found going on about 'arresting someone for murder or another for breaking and entering, trespass and whatever else followed', trying now to act like forgetting she'd spoken to

Danny and Ray again in her imagination.

"I *have* seen a lot of strange stuff Greg, as a police officer in an prolonged overnight coma is sometimes known to."
"Unlike that little bastard who probably *took* too much of it."
"*How long* have I been unconscious?"
"Fifteen hours, I already told you, but don't worry about that now. Fifteen *days* would've made us wonder a little."

Garstone tried to keep things light knowing that he had little choice other than to accept defeat from his bed-ridden superior, who it seemed had seen as much with her eyes shut as she usually did with them open. As he strove to begin the banter in earnest, the curtain   ruffled back slightly.

"Detective Inspector Leyton?" one of the young nurses put her head through then suddenly receded again a moment "oh excuse me, make that *Acting Detective Superintendent* Leyton - sorry to disturb you but a Mr Armstrong's on the phone."
"Thanks, and by the way you'll find its Mr *Armitage,* you met just then."
"Here, I'll take it."

Not allowing time to congratulate Leyton right then, Garstone bounced straight out through the curtain, and then just behind it his tone suddenly brightened.

"Thought you might eventually find where she was hiding. All yours, lads."

Leyton didn't have time to ponder who he had suddenly met outside, as the two other people she'd hoped to see more than any other right now stood at the end of her bed. Robbie Draycott, impressively subdued again like as if yesterday's emotional explosion had never happened, was one person definitely unused to being in hospital as a visitor rather than a patient, with Ray having to remind him that the beds in the ward were not for his regular form of use this time round.

"I'm afraid he's a patient too, now." Ray smiled, showing slight embarrassment. "Want to show her your 'scratch', Rob?"
"I believe I've already seen it, "Leyton stopped him as he lifted his woolly hat aside.
"It took an entire day to let me see it."
"Was scared, wasn't I?" Robbie excused himself freely but modestly.
"Oh Rob, you silly sausage, you had us more scared than everyone."
"*You're* scared?" Ray didn't want Robbie to sound forgiven "It wasn't that much of a pretty sight for me either, let alone the potential Health & Safety roasting, I thankfully won't be facing any longer."
"Go on, what's the story."
"Oh, he just tried playing *Kenny Everett* with the tyre cutter...didn't we, young man?"
"Really?"

Leyton, in her aching bed-ridden state, struggled with all but short lines but in knowing quietness embraced Ray's story, so honestly put and straight point enough to ingest. She leant her head across to Robbie as a lengthier one naturally flowed with the moment.

"Aw Robbie," she laughed, hating to be firm "you must learn to do what your Uncle Ray tells you. You should see the trouble that using individual technique got me into, with Mr Hargreaves."
"Who's he?" Ray asked, looking slightly guilty for am moment here "I thought I knew him but not sure."
"You don't want to," Leyton stopped Robbie as he lent to remind

his employer quietly by ear "In short, call him our second biggest problem after Bennington."

Tired as she may have been, Leyton found it might be the only time to share the truth with both of them at the same time about what her DCS had actually done to Robbie and what she'd then gone on to do to the evil man himself.

"Horrible man!" gasped Ray "I so wish he was up there with that little Bennington brute, or down below, more like; both were as bad as the other in my book."
"Where's Danny Bennington gone up to?" Robbie became excited.
"Danny's dead, Robbie, as no one's got around to mentioning it yet."
"Really? Who did it? The murderer?"
"Er, yeah, suppose."
"Aw, Ray," Leyton came to his rescue "I think you'd better explain to Robbie on the way home what some people, like Danny Bennington, prefer to do rather than waiting to face the brunt of the law."
"Would you be ok if I get it over with right away?"

Ray sat his young protégé down and quietly talked him through Danny Bennington's fate. Unlike the previous death he'd heard about this weekend, Robbie was fighting laughter this time, though unintentionally raised it from the rest by asking who the person called 'Brunt of The Law' was. The entire atmosphere, an absolute contrast to that of 24 hours previous created a real Christmas-like feel in the room, as if everyone shared new beginnings.

"Good. I'm glad he's dead." Robbie turned serious his look on, towards Leyton again "Pity about the lots of people he killed."
"But he missed me and you." Ray summarised "'Chavs' -

whatever you prefer to call them - target both our sort, day in day out so we did quite well in that respect."

"I think 'Chav's a little too nice for Danny Bennington right now." Leyton rubbed it in for comfort "Another 'C' word comes to mind, though."

Leyton wasn't exactly all for enforcing the obligations of political correctness from her casualty ward bed. Ray found time to laugh together with Robbie for the first moment today. As the DI caught herself sniggering as well, Garstone reappeared.

"Looks like our time's up," Ray acknowledged his presence.

"No, stay." Garstone told him "The two-to-a-bed rule doesn't apply with police."

"Thanks Mr Garstone but we'd better be moving. You two have the catching up -I've got the hard day at the garage. Take care."

"You too." Leyton smiled "Robbie, you look after him, now."

"Of course he will, even though my boy needs looking after himself, heh heh."

Leyton waited till they had gone, Robbie turning back to wave every time Ray moved him along, before continuing.

"That was a quick chat; distinctively below your usual thirty-minutes-minimum."

"Well it didn't even need two for him to lay it down. Danny did top himself - just as you thought."

"I didn't *think* it Greg- I knew it for a fact."

"Well our other man's clarified it. The wrench we found on the floor inside, presumed used on your head and Gipton's was also the same sort Ray himself would keep around him for pulling awkward metal stuff apart."

"Including his garage chains?"

"That's what we believe."

Garstone, in absolutely no literal terms confirmed that the chains Danny Bennington used were the exact set Ray bound nightly to his shutter. Adding this with the rest, all the signs of a suicide were intact. *Danny had basically premeditated ending it right there, realising all his exits were blocked.* Her level of reflectivity impressed him as she laboured through the anecdote.

"Shows you've proven your worth as acting DCS in just one day.' already."
"I suppose."
"You certainly didn't miss anything; the sort he had takes about twenty seconds min' to cut across, and that's just using the best Black-And-Deckers."

(That time would have meant nothing at all to Danny,) as Garstone went on, explaining to his bed-ridden boss. (*HE carried the weapon HE created the 'noose'. Making himself a length, Danny sought privacy in the back room, placed the end through the wall-hook, then kicked away the chair)*

"You sound strangely unimpressed, ma'am."
"I've been wondering since you took that call."

A frosty expression shrouded her - the kind that usually unnerved Garstone too.

"One or two things look... well I'd say frankly rather uneven."
"What, no chair?"
"There probably was one, but that was when we dropped in two days ago."
"What is it you're trying to say, apart from *there's a problem with me agreeing with you,* all of a sudden?"
"It's simple," Layton finished her water before bombing him with worse than sporadic spit. "Danny didn't kill himself."

"It wasn't him."

Leyton broke her silence on the subject again, the first time since sat at the table. The school-diner drabness of the A&E canteen added a darkening air as two detectives took their bedside discussion to shed some light. With the place otherwise deserted Leyton had the privacy to shout if she needed, only the room was so cold with also the lack of additional bodies around to generate heat that lip movement also became hard. She eventually forced her effort for the warmth left in her large cocoa and teacake.

"What?" Garstone ached to know, as always.
"I've just been thinking a little."
"*Aye,* can happen when you've been lying in here, half a day with your lights knocked out. Go on, try doing the same to me then, wonder woman."
"I walked in on Ray threatening to relieve Danny of his head - I can only recall being promptly rewarded with a blow the back of my head."

The only explanation she could root it down to was the preposterous thought of Danny owning an 'Inspector Gadget'-style mechanical arm that extended secretly round the edge of the workshop, collecting a blunt item somewhere along.

"You expect the department to stand on that?"
"What else then?" (*If the very last thing I saw was those two fighting till the death right in front of my eyes, then unless something poorly secured dropped on me from the ceiling, what the hell have I left to suspect?*)

Realising the cashier was listening she supped her cocoa and rescued her cool just slightly faster than back at the station yesterday afternoon. And again, like the, her right hand man was ready to jump back in.

"You were knocked out from behind... is that what you're on about?" Garstone prodded it out from her.
"Another point goes to Mr G. Yes, for the third time, when I got there, he had Danny in a headlock, straight there; right opposite me. Now I'm fooled by many things Greg but the myth of teleportation is still far back in that old queue."

The discussion for all its repetitive monotony had finally added in its missing dimension. Using Bennington's imaginary ability to- double himself to both sides of the shop as the starting point, it was straightforward enough to replace… with a fourth party in the room.

Leyton's assault was no less of manual nature than Danny's. The ceiling being too low to accommodate any realistic booby trap, Ray could have fit something just recently, expecting guests, but she would have activated it on immediate entry.

This turned their additional figure into a frightful definiteness though possibilities rested that split the scenario open wide. Bennington may have had an accomplice in waiting who'd seen to both of them. With neither Ray nor Leyton seeming likely to ever get up again Danny saw, in full reality the line he'd hoped never to cross. Hence the suicide - again possibly assisted unless this 'fourth' had run, caring just for his own bacon.

Had Ray been lured to his attack as well? His reflexes on the sight of Leyton dropping to the floor in a heap must have incurred him to release Danny - the 'fourth' would have struck Ray as he was trying to revive her. An old police favourite Leyton had seen as basis for random murders aplenty, logics became crossed here that made it ineffective.

The best tale written for now read: the 'Fourth' attacked Leyton, then turned straight onto Ray, who had released 'Burglar Bennington' before he, himself being claimed in the resulting struggle. With both down, and blood beginning to run, this only left Danny to deal with. The 'Fourth', if a vigilant enough criminal, would have ventured straight to the back without fail and cornered the boy there, with no window for Bennington to climb through.

But then again what could Ray have been up to once Leyton had been incapacitated? Garstone had one last approach: he wasn't about to contain it, though diplomacy did beckon.

"I don't know if he actually touched Danny with it but the Stanley was the same make."
"Yes, I noticed that too, thus the ultimatum."
"Is this the thing about a choice between pulling Gipton for murder or him for..."
"That's right. *Plu-us* one more thing I remember - that song...'Round and Round'".
[*You were looking at one of his heavy metal tapes when we visited. That track was just starting as I cornered them - my ex-boyfriend used to have the album it was on.)* Do you still remember that expression?"
"Aye, the thing that dead guy was chanting at Green Oak - also made Robbie destroy half a funfair, right?"
"Yes, well took down the canopy of a duck stall - the real point is that now either an audible broadcast *or* distinct physical representation of this phrase attracts the killer to his victim. (*So he, whoever he is turned up at Ray's yesterday, to find Danny also kitted out just like one of them, and 'bang'!)*"
"You think Danny spotted someone else in the pub who wanted a word? Perhaps *Hargreaves* was hiding in a corner somewhere?"

"Well there could be plenty around baying for Danny's blood, but nothing's possible to put money on just yet."

"Apart from in here, right?"

Garstone craned up at the waiting room TV just outside. The headline '*SHEFFIELD YOUTH'S SUICIDE IN PANIC*' scrolled across the red at the bottom, followed by '*Boy 18, Feared Arrest After Knocking Cop Unconscious*' beckoned to be read out loud.

"*O-h-h* dear." Leyton laughed it off "That'll cause some red faces in the Star office."

"You're dead certain aren't you?"

"Excuse me," whispered Sister o'Reardon as she suddenly swung herself through the curtain, "Are either of you two friends of Mr Gipton by any chance?"

"Aye, suppose you could say that."

"There's been a wallet found on the floor in the A & E ward. I'm wondering if either of you two could be so kind as to verify it as his."

"I think I'd better let my trusty errand boy see to that, eh?" she nudged Garstone.

"Yeah, otherwise you'll be making about twenty calls for each card you find inside... not even being in hospital keeps you off police work, does it?"

Correct as usual he was on that account - as soon as he had turned his back, Leyton was making straight for the payphone in the lobby. Looking round the side to make sure he'd not followed, she rang the Midelson office number like a maniac, getting an understandably flat reception from her other DC down the line.

"Christ pal, you could have let us get meself back in the station."

"That's an interesting way of pronouncing 'Hello ma'am, glad to hear you're alright', I must say."

"Hey up, ma'am, right sorry about that. How's thee now, any road?"

"Not that bad thanks. The collarbone is requiring another night of observation, otherwise just bruises to beware of."

"Listen, I just got back in and…"

"So you were just saying. Regrettably, on how Greg's just spelt things you're going to have to go a-l-l-ll the way back again - taking with you that wonderful blue tape saying *murder scene'*."

"Eh…?"

Armitage dropped to that guilty slur, carrying on before Leyton was able to get her foot in the door again.

"It were just what Greg and the lads believed at the scene, because of how the chain were set up, and that."

"So your chinwag with him earlier was intended just to put you in the picture was it?"

Leyton realised this discussion was of little use - other than to lighten her purse by a few excessive 20p pieces.

"'Do you think I could have a chat wi' him myself - if he's still there?"

"Jo!" a sudden cry from round the corner.

"I think he wants one with *me* again."

Leyton terminated the chat politely, scooting back to the canteen as fast as her loosely oversized hospital slippers supported. Her DC met her out in the corridor, nursing her cocoa.

"Best sit down but don't make yourself too comfy." he helped her into a vacant office opposite. "To say, this is pretty big, like…."

He emptied Gipton's wallet across the table like playing cards for a poker game, spreading them apart just enough for clarity.

"What are we supposed to be seeing?" Leyton asked, totally a mental vegetable right now.
"That for a start."

Garstone put one nearer her, a faded PhotoHut 3x2 showing Ray of about 10 years before. It instantly rang bells; one of the various things she caught him moseying over whilst there on Thursday morning, not satisfied with probing Ray's rock n' roll collection. While appreciative that the other one of the set sat on his worktop corner, fully coloured as opposed to a pitiful dirge of darkening greens and whites, it still didn't shoot anything useful out towards her.

"Hold it a bit closer, Jo, there's something you're missing here. Probably murder to make out with the fade, but worth trying."

Leyton hadn't actually had a proper a look but duly went along with his theory.

"Hmm." she approved of the mechanic's previous look "He also appears to have had a moustache in his younger days."
"Aye, so did someone else, *very* temporarily."
"That's tru… Hey, hold on - that shirt!"

Leyton's jaw hit the ground as she studied the younger Ray's attire closer, honing her overtly fluent skills in colour detection. Piles of comics she'd hoarded over the years in her dad's loft had decayed into shades of blue and green with age. Putting the same principle into practice, the sweater would have been red in real life in order to adopt that olive tint throughout the photo's slow deterioration. Another picture was now developing in both detectives' heads, although invisible to one another's.

215

"Hey you know another thing, ma'am. You said 'Round and Round' being on, attracted him to the scene… you think he might just have sprung out, only to find you in the way?"
"Who?"
"Ray… I mean… the killer."
"RAY?!"

"That just slipped out." Garstone tried to cancel out his use of Ray Gipton's name from that line.
"Whether it did or not," Leyton however agreed, "think about what we're looking at here."

She pushed one of Ray's calling cards right in front of him. The tyre rack symbol jumped out and struck him right there and then. *The 'A' logo!* The two shapes were almost identical. Garstone paired the 'tube sign' from Jon Cloughton's body up alongside it for some seconds, before silently dismissing it - it was still a contrastable standout, alongside to even the poorest of eyes.

"Oh my g…"

Leyton jolted straight up, looking down at the Gipton card closely.

"It fits right down to the finger, Greg. All five men - *six*, if Danny's short-lived incognito stint counts - match closely with Ray's previous look. Imposters aside, Mr Cloughton's easily the closest to a dead ringer so far, though the average murderer seldom allows time to distinguish a fake moustache in the dark."
"Aye, there's something there."

Garstone looked and thought deeper. More shapes slotted into even more holes here. Ray Gipton had been clean-shaven only for about a year at the longest but could have worn that moustache for up to twenty years, maybe longer even. His old

216

image was clearly iconic but he wasn't too pleased at people mocking it, along with having the nerve to break into his workshop to prove a point.

"There's also the car tracks too." Leyton added, as if by magic seeing her other lead reappear in her head.
"Aye, if it was him he was not alone."
"I knew that already, silly-socks. We cleared that up at the scene."
"We discussed those well-spaced-out footprints of yours. Still means only one guy behind the other couple."
"Most people bring others grapes in hospital, Greg: you just like bringing arguments." "You've left the first two murders almost out of the equation, in your dithering over the Bennington business."
"Don't worry I haven't, but the logo is our only threat though the entire set."

Ecclesby and Mc Mahon's murders seemed already like a set of two within a bigger six but 'one' seemed wrong now for the number of culprits in the earlier crimes. Yes, Ray in his trade would be used to a bit of muck on the tyres, so trawling it across a mushy playing field was quite second nature. The fact that there were no tracks discovered in Dore or Green Oak could be explained without saying, as the waters showed up a neatly un-muddied side.

To ensure a quick enough escape, one guy would have had to be backing the car up ready again, but with both parks barriers shut, getting a vehicle through wasn't going to be a quick enough move. Leyton remembered some sports ground or other adjoining the Rec. Robbie had reported at the time as having found its gate forced slightly apart moments before he discovered Ecclesby himself – a fact ignored by Hargreaves, back at the time but still a likely failed attempt to bring the car through from another way originally. Either one or two men could be placed behind the crime; it had just turned thrice harder for Garstone to give Leyton the version she'd prefer.

"Okay, ma'am, there were two of them, if you like. But whether Mr Gipton's either half of the dirty duo, still can't be picked at for definite."
"I just didn't want to jump to conclusions."

Leyton had maintained an undetected lump in her gut at the thought of apprehending Ray Gipton for murder. Again, it just made less sense than none that Ray would be behind this callous string of crimes. Ray Gipton, the man who could hardly turn to face Leyton when he first spoke to her on Thursday. Ray Gipton, a man on the verge of tears at anyone else's unjust misfortunes, friends or otherwise. Ray, a man who never shouted at anybody, notably Robbie, the friend he saw as a son.

That final entry separated the loose ends all over again, like a duff coupling between carriages. Watching the way they came in to visit her, arm placed round Robbie's shoulder, all the way and his visibly mortified expression, on seeing the friendliest police officer he'd ever met lying in a hospital bed. Even if he was also the last person to have seen Danny alive, who could accept that it was Ray and not that fictitious accomplice who'd been responsible?

"Look, ma'am, if it's Ray, it's Ray." Garstone still brought it out of her, "I thought he was a sound chap myself, but since when has that stopped anyone from becoming a serial killer?"
"We've still got to stop him before he gets back there."

She shot out into the corridor, conveniently finding Sister O'Reardon walking up.

"Excuse me, did you see what time Mr Gipton and Mr Draycott left?"

"About half an hour ago, love." Sister O'Reardon replied in her typical motherly manner, "They got into a taxi outside."

"Oh god. Greg, the car!!!!"

"Hey aren't you supposed to be a patient of this hospital for another day?" Garstone was inevitably bewildered by her intent.

"*You* will be if we aren't out of that car park within thirty seconds!" She pointed him towards the glass double doors "Choose the right route and we may just get in front."

Abbeydale Road was still *hopefully* cut up by various roadworks till halfway out of the city, if she remembered rightly from Friday's journey.

"God, I hope we got this right about Ray." worried Garstone, "No disrespect but if he finds himself being nicked by a woman in a nightie, people are gonna talk."

(iii)

For all her efforts to settle the agreement, 'arrest' wasn't a word Leyton really wished to hear or use in dealing with Ray Gipton of all people. The strong believer in innocent-till-proven-guilty she was, Ray's reserved persona still forbade her to accept such a soft-hearted individual would be capable of brutally murdering six men, regardless of his movements in tackling Bennington.

Garstone ignored her body language, as they shot down Spital Hill but he knew what he saw. Neither spoke for another five minutes but Leyton, however, was rapidly ironing out the creases. Even the DC's counterproductively carefree manoeuvres

219

as he torpedoed across the town centre ring roads didn't meet the absolute top of her concern-o-meter this very minute.

"Greg…. no, no forget it."

On beginning to say something difficult, she finished. The biggest elephant in the room was too hard to move without her becoming trampled on. She didn't like to say so but Ray had no alibi for any of the scenes. That Danny Bennington died in his garage last night seemed unhappily substantial for Leyton's case - Ray just coincidentally working a Saturday night out of the blue like that.

One major part had already made its stay in the story, 'Round and Round', the ghastly line linked to four out of these six crimes - be that either *cause* of the crime, *during* the crime or even *inspired by* the crime.   Peeping from the edge of the circumstantial pile, the fact still lingered that the last three all involved items they knew to be used by Ray- even without reappearance of 'A' or 'Tube Sign' last night, the case was nauseatingly damning against Ray Gipton by now.

(*Killer is lured by the sweet sound of 'Round and Round', standing inside is this young man hurtfully lampooning Ray's heyday looks*) Oh how that theory rode straight out of the window, behind all last dementia Leyton still might harbour.

So yes, Ray was impelled by revenge but also restrained by the lack of balls to take a young lad's life himself - thus enter the 'fourth', a now-existent myth to assist him with the job. This would mean the trap was set for Bennington and Bennington alone; that song had been chosen as his friend's cue to move from hiding, wrench in hand. (Last *thing they wanted right then was an uppity cop crashing in on them*)

"You know something?" Garstone intruded on her delusions once again.

"Go on..." she didn't sound too desperate to listen but tried.

"That logo, you know, the 'A' thing he leaves behind each time."

"Hmmmm?"

"You think you've never seen that shape anyplace else?"

"I can't say."

"Try it more from the side. What do you get now... - and *don't* say 'Masons'?"

"Well, a swing, amongst others."

An idiot would guess rightly at the circle representing the motion of the swing seat, yet this being drawn a full 360-degree lap, it might have even been based on one such type that travelled the full distance over.

"Robbie's mum claimed he'd picked up his crippling injury, falling off a…"

"Off a swing, yes..."

Leyton didn't mind his riddles but whatever Garstone was trying to entertain her with here, it had better come quick as they were now three minutes drive from putting Ray Gipton in a pair of handcuffs.

"Now…" he decided to test her "What does he do every morning at about seven o'clock til eight?"

"Well I can't really vouch for Ray, but Robbie goes out for a run. I told you that already, I thought - as had his mother."

"Aye, a run. What can you picture? Go on."

"Only my Detective Constable spouting out a pile of directionless yarn." She made it clear that her bearings weren't quite fully back in following the knock she'd taken last night. "It still says just about *nothing* to me, Greg. For God's sake, when we take him in, just read him his rights and let me do the rest, or better still leave it all to Leroy."

"Speaking of whom..."

"*GREG! MA'AM! In here, quick! Leave the car!*"

A figure they both just had time to recognise as DC Armitage hollered frantically running along the middle of Penny Lane, arms flaying if trying to guide down an out-of-control plane.

"Looks like Ray's already figured the flying squad are over." Garstone pretended aloud, keeping his beliefs of the moment discreet, "if he's creating the scene I'm getting the impression of."

"I would have too Greg had I been there already."

Leyton still didn't fully side with him but had no time to lay down firm decisions as she found herself hurried through this wall of woodland for the third time in about as many days. A gathering of flashing blue beacons she knew only too well lured her diving through the fence, overtaken by Garstone, always intent to be first to the line. Not allowing time to adjust her brace, caught on the car door's side she cannoned along towards where officer, after officer directed her. The final uniform was standing right outside the wide-open shutter of No 1 Tall Trees Farm.

"Ma'am! Greg!" yelled PC Collins from outside Ray's entrance. "In here!"

"You'd better stay back, ma'am." warned Thompson stepping in "Given how unstable he seems, he could lash out without telling friend from foe!"

Falling on closed ears as normal, he was brushed aside by Leyton as she battled her way in. Her heart stopped as she did on entering the clearing at the back of the shop. In fact, she felt it sink like a cricket ball in a bowlful of custard.

"Robbie… Oh no, please don't say you've…"

The young man stood breathing over Ray's body. A pool of deep red fluid trickled from the left of the mechanic's neck, following down the line of his collar onto the floor. Leyton stepped back as it picked up its pace along the tiles towards her. As she quietly warned Garstone back as well, Robbie began breathing heavily. He let go of the yellow Pro-cut which clattered to the ground, distributing the stream of crimson wider.

He breathed louder, now moving into rhythm. His lips began to move.

"*Round and round…*" could just be heard, whispered.

Leyton looked at Garstone as if she suddenly understood something new, but it fell out from reach of speaking.

"*Round and round…*" Robbie repeated again, slightly louder and as doing so, looked at them both. "*Round and Round….*"
It got a degree louder with progressive repeats, a frightening smile assembling on Robbie's face.
"*Round and round… Round and round.*"

Leyton couldn't stand it, ramming the palms of her hands into her ears as he screamed it at a rhythm by now incessant.

"*ROUND AND ROUND …ROUND AND ROUND!*"

She shut her eyes as well but it wouldn't stop.

"*ROUND AND ROUND…ROUND AND ROUND!!!! ROUND AND ROUND…ROUND AND ROUND!!!! ROUND AND ROUND…ROUND AND ROUND!!!!*"

End.

FIONA

by Dave Attrill

A young woman runs riot through a busy shopping precinct, a cyclist is badly injured in a hit and run, a cleaner is found murdered on a motorway footbridge. All three incidents in one day, within one small corner of the city sees DI Leyton's day seems busy enough already only for her one-time Cambridge room-mate Becky to re-appear into her life. Finding her work as a nanny to a friendly young Scottish single mum, Leyton and Garstone commit again to the cases, unaware that the clues slowly unearthed link to a deadly background story while Becky's new employer slowly un-shields a dark side. Time against them, a ticking human bomb imprisons Leyton's friend as the detectives amble on possibly unconvinced, till the last moment of the dangers others face. *Based partly on a true story.*

(Available: late 2011)